THE
HEALER

MARK B. HONEYCUTT

THE HEALER

Copyright © Mark B. Honeycutt, 2012
All rights reserved.

LIBRARY OF CONGRESS
CATALOGING IN PUBLICATION DATA
ISBN -10: 0-9882291-1-0
ISBN -13: 978-0-9882291-1-2

Printed in the United States of America
Set in Palatino Linotype
Designed by Sherry L. Honeycutt

Chapter 1

The storm followed the four horsemen as they galloped up the narrow mountain road. Billowing black clouds rolled and crashed behind them, pushed by winds that stirred the dusty soil, making it impossible to see very well. A bolt of lightning flashed violently at the edge of the front, exploding into a tall pine above them. The tree toppled down the cliff, hitting the road before it fell end-over-end into the valley below just a few seconds before they rounded the bend.

Artus knew this was no ordinary storm. They'd been chased for hours by the Sarcugian guards, and this weather was nothing more than Druck's doing. The Sarcugian's were fierce warriors, but he knew he and his men could take them. They were the Emperor's elite guard, and they'd spent their lives preparing for these moments. They weren't, however, prepared to fight a magician, especially one as powerful as Druck, so they rode hard, trying to pull away from the magic before it overtook them.

The three soldiers pulled their horses to a quick stop after they rounded the bend. The horses slid through the sandy soil, barely coming to a halt before the steep slope that marked the end of the road. Artus grabbed the reins of the fourth horse and pulled hard to keep it from going over the edge. Its rider, Lord Nilet, was barely conscious. As his horse stepped unsteadily down the slope, the tall, elderly lord slid forward in the saddle and landed on top of the horse's neck. His purple cloak flew in the air and covered his horse's head, panicking the stallion as it tried to gain its footing on the uneven ground. It reared onto its hind legs and threw him onto the road.

Artus calmed the horse and pulled it towards him. It was as important to Lord Nilet's survival as was his head right now, so he wanted to secure the stallion before checking on the old man. He took the horse back to his two men who had turned around to guard against any forward threat. With swords raised, they struggled to control their nervous stallions as they pranced unsteadily in the loose soil.

"Take this," said Artus while handing the reins to Kiro. He whirled his horse around and turned back towards Lord Nilet. "And keep your eyes out!" he shouted. "We're no more than an hour ahead of them."

Kiro grabbed the reins and glanced at the magician. He gripped his sword and wiped sweat off his forehead with the back of his hand. It was hot, his tongue was caked with dirt, and they were low on water, so he was as anxious to get back to Gornia as quickly as possible. "Let them have him," he mumbled. When he looked up, he saw a patch of green below the cliff. Squinting, he was able to make out a snaking river. It was the Elbe! "The border!" he shouted. "Look, Captain, we've made it!"

Artus didn't bother to look. He already knew where they were, and he was well aware of the difficult journey ahead of them. The Sarcugian road ended here, a result of the peace treaty between Sarcus and Gornia over a hundred years ago. There was only one road leading into Gornia, and it was over two hundred legions west of their current location. While a useful remedy to limit contact between both countries, it created a problem for them because they would have to take their already tired horses on a journey over unstable ground full of rocks, holes, and possibly traps.

Artus' knees buckled when he dismounted his horse. He'd been in the saddle for a long time, and the weight of his armor sank into his fatigued legs making him feel unsteady on the ground. The years were catching up to him, he thought, and he questioned why he'd been ordered to lead this mission. Instead of being chased by a garrison of Sarcugian cavalry and Druck's black magic, he thought a life guarding the Emperor's wives as they took their leisure in the bathhouse suited him better. But here he was nonetheless, and he had to find a way out of Druck's reach as quickly as possible. The border wasn't a guarantee, though, and he knew it. Druck might choose to pursue them into Gornia even if it meant war.

He rolled Lord Nilet onto his back and cradled the magician's head in his arms. Uncorking his canteen, he slowly poured the last few ounces of water into the old man's mouth. Lord Nilet was barely conscious enough to swallow, and he seemed to be unaware of the predicament they were in. Artus unbuckled the clasp that held the purple cloak around the old man's neck. Usually, this would not be possible. No one was allowed to unclasp a magician's cloak other than a magician, but this was not the time or the place to worry about such things. The cloak's gold chain was wrapped tightly around his neck, and Artus knew he needed to get it off soon so the magician could breathe.

"Thank you," whispered the old man. He cracked his eyelids open wide enough for Artus to see his blue eyes as they darted back and forth. Lord Nilet reached up and put his hand over Artus' neck. His forehead filled with concern as he tried to focus on the captain's blurry face. "Are we in Tarsus?" His hand slipped off Artus' sweaty neck and landed on his chest.

"No, my Lord," said Artus. He placed two fingers over Lord Nilet's neck and felt his heart beat. "We're still in Sarcus." He turned his head to look behind his two men. The clouds rolled steadily towards them as the wind gusts got stronger. The Sarcugians were closing in, and he knew they had to keep moving in order to survive. "They're getting close, and we need to get out of here. Can you make it?"

Lord Nilet turned towards Artus. Although caked with dust, the magician's white beard glistened in the last few rays of sunlight. "Leave me to Druck," he said. "I'll slow you down."

"My Lord, we can't leave you!" yelled Artus. "You're the only one who knows what Druck is planning. If he has you, then thousands of Gornians will die in his dungeons, and I won't let that happen." He rolled the purple cloak into a ball and laid Lord Nilet's head on top of it while he thought.

"Captain!" yelled Kiro. He pointed at the ridge they crossed thirty minutes before. "They're approaching quickly. We're only five legions ahead of them."

Artus looked south. The clouds hovered over the ridge, and the thick mountain trees swayed back and forth as the wind whipped them around like tiny saplings. "We've got to go!" he shouted. "Bring me the horse. I'll tie him to the saddle if I have to."

Kiro spurred his horse forward and handed the

reins to Artus. He bent over towards his Captain. "Let's just leave him to those animals," he whispered nervously. "We can get out of here, but if we take him with us, there's no guarantee."

Artus' face wrinkled with anger. He drew his sword and stuck it under Kiro's neck, pushing the point into the soldier's skin. Kiro grimaced and slowly sat up in his saddle as Artus pushed on his blade. "That's treason!" yelled Artus. He jabbed the sword a little harder, pushing the edge into Kiro's neck. "Do you understand how important he is, you fool?! We're getting him back alive!"

A stream of blood rolled down Kiro's neck, turning the edge of his wet collar red. He twisted his head as far away from the blade as he could. "Captain, please accept my apology," he gargled. "I...I meant no disrespect." Artus' blade was now deeply underneath his skin, and it burned badly as the sweat and dirt trickled into the open wound. "I wasn't thinking. It won't happen again." He closed his eyes and prayed that Artus wouldn't run him through. "It won't happen again, I said!" he pleaded.

Artus looked towards the approaching Sarcugians. He shook his head and slowly pulled his sword out of Kiro's neck. "Apology accepted." He turned Lord Nilet's horse around and walked towards the magician. "Let's get him ready to ride. Dismount and help me get him back on the damn horse."

Kiro wiped his neck and sheathed his sword, before getting off his mount. The magician looked weak, and he wasn't sure he'd make the journey. He wouldn't dare cross Artus again, though. That would be certain death.

The two men lifted Lord Nilet onto the horse, and Artus tied his hands to the pommel with a rope. He picked up the magician's cloak and mounted his horse.

"What are you going to do with that?" asked Kiro. It was a crime for a mortal to be in possession of a magician's cloak.

"I'm not keeping it, if that's what you mean," said Artus. He moved his horse close to Lord Nilet and clasped the chain around his neck. "He might need this before this is over." Artus grabbed the reins of both horses and moved to the slope's edge. "Let's move!" he yelled. He prodded his horse with his spurs, leaned back in the saddle, and started down the steep hill. Kiro and Rogeris followed closely behind.

After ten long minutes of slow descent, they reached the dark soil of the river basin and rode into the lush forest separating the mountains from the Elbe River. It was a hard, grinding ride because the forest was full of Partica, a bush indigenous to southern Gornia known for its spiky thorns. The thick thorns tore into their legs and their horses' sides, making a bloody mess of them all. Artus drew his sword and tried to clear a path, but it wouldn't cut through the fibrous bushes. He stopped his horse and looked west. "There's a clearing over there," he said, pointing his sword in the direction he wanted to go. "We'll see if we have better luck there." He knew their time was running out, and cutting a path through the thorns was costing them too much.

The clearing turned out to be an old road that ran into the river. It was the final leg of the road that ended at the cliff and was probably forgotten about once the Sarcugian magicians blasted the mountain after the war. It was the main slave route into Sarcus, and Gornia insisted the road be closed after winning the long-fought war.

Artus and Lord Nilet arrived at the road as the two other guards came out of the thicket. "We're fortunate," said Artus. "This will take us right to the Elbe. Then it's only a couple of legions to Heshire."

"Heshire?" asked Rogeris while pulling a thorn from his thigh. He winced in pain when the thick thorn came out. "I thought we were going directly to Tarsus."

"If we don't get new mounts, we'll never make it. We need the rest as well," he said while looking at the sky. The clouds were closing in quickly. They had been slowed down too much, and they needed to get moving. "Lord Barton rules Heshire. Perhaps he can help Lord Nilet."

Kiro looked at the old magician. "Is he alive?"

"Barely," said Artus. He turned his horse south and punched his spurs into the stallion's side. "Let's go!" he shouted.

The old road hadn't been used in years, so the soil was thick with deep sand, which slowed the tired horses even more. Saplings and small bushes grew in the middle of the road, but it was nothing compared to the pesky Partica bushes they'd fought in the thicket.

Lightning flashed over their heads and rain began to fall, finally catching up with them after the ten-hour chase. Artus pulled his horse to a stop and turned to look. At the top of the hill where they'd stopped to regroup earlier, he finally saw the Sarcugian horsemen who'd been chasing them since they left Druck's castle the night before. Even through the driving rain, he could see their formidable silhouettes against the sky. Their black armor and chainmail with hoods that shadowed their faces, made them look as evil as they were.

The three were ready to ride into the river when Artus saw him. He wore a black robe with a black magician's cloak, and he held a long staff.

Artus turned to his men. "It's Druck!" he shouted. "We've got to get over that river now!"

"What's he doing?" shouted Kiro. He wiped the rain from his face and shielded his eyes in order to get a better look.

Artus moved behind both men. It was not the time to gawk. Druck was close enough to kill them. "Move it!" he ordered, and he galloped down the muddy road.

The Sarcugian soldiers watched from the top of the mountain as the Gornian's rode towards the river. The captain of the garrison turned to Druck. "My Lord," he said. "Do you want us to engage them?"

Druck looked at his captain with eyes that burned like fire. "No. I'll take it from here." He turned back and stared at the fleeing horsemen. He had them where he wanted, and it was time to end this chase once and for all. "No one steals from me," he said. "Not even you, Nilet." He knew the old magician could hear him. He sensed it just as he sensed the magician's true intentions the night before.

Druck raised his staff high above his head. A bolt of lightning struck the round crystal in the top of his staff. He laughed as electricity coursed harmlessly into the ground. The lightning strike spooked his soldier's horses, throwing many to the ground and causing the rest of them to ride in circles as they calmed their mounts. The dark magician looked back and smiled. These mortals know nothing of magic, he thought. He turned around with eyes that swirled in red. "Mortum, Pristis, Cardicum." The crystal glowed, and a beam of bright light shot towards the fleeing riders.

As Druck uttered the incantation, Lord Nilet sat high in his saddle. Although his body was weak, his magical awareness was strong, and he sensed the attack. "Harthog, Harthog, Andulantium," he muttered before he lost consciousness and fell over.

The strong beam struck the four horsemen hard, knocking them off their horses and sending them to the ground. Lord Nilet was able to cast a protective spell against Druck's magic before he passed out, but it only provided partial protection due to his weakened condition. It was enough to keep them alive for now, but there were no guarantees beyond that.
Artus was thrown into a shrub not far from Lord Nilet. As soon as he hit the ground, he felt his stomach burn. He looked down and saw a small hole about the size of a coin in his breastplate. The burn went all the way to the skin. He patted the hole to put out the embers around the edges of the armor, and he jumped to his feet to check on everyone else.

Kiro and Rogeris rolled on the ground screaming. They were behind Artus and Lord Nilet, receiving the brunt of the impact as a result. Artus ran to his men and pulled off their breastplates and chainmail. Both were burned so severely that their armor, chainmail, and shirts were completely gone at the back. Thinking the downpour wasn't enough to calm their burns, he scooped water from a puddle and frantically doused their backs.

"We're dead!" yelled Kiro. "We shouldn't have taken the old man!"

Artus wasn't about to argue with him right now, especially after he'd been injured so badly. He looked around and saw that their horses were killed by the impact. The rear of their mounts had been incinerated all the way up to the saddles, making it look like they'd been cut in half by a heavy blade.

"I want you to take our horses and ride to Heshire. There's a healer there who'll take care of you." He looked towards the cliff. The Sarcugians were gone. But the rain was still falling hard, so he knew they were on their way to finish them off. "Tell Lord Barton that Lord Nilet is trapped. Tell him to send his guards immediately."

The two men nodded their heads. They clambered to their feet and climbed on top of the two remaining horses, slowly trotting down the road towards the Elbe.

Artus turned around and staggered to Lord Nilet who was lying motionless on the ground. He rolled the magician over and felt his pulse. "Still alive," he mumbled. "Now let's get ourselves to a safer place." He grabbed the old man underneath the armpits and dragged him into the thicket, hiding behind a large boulder about a hundred paces from the road. He sat Lord Nilet against the rock and dropped beside him, holding his sword in one hand and rubbing his stomach with the other. "If you can hear me, my Lord, we could use a little magic right now," he said.

The elder magician grabbed Artus' hand tightly

but didn't speak. Artus looked at him. "I knew you were still in there somewhere."

Chapter 2

Healing someone with a fever was a difficult proposition, especially when the person was barely conscious. It took time to determine the cause. Aidan knew that because he'd seen his father treat many people with similar symptoms through the years, and it seemed to take a different method each time to cure the sickness. The fevers were getting worse over the past few months, and no one, not even his father, understood why.

The girl's mother stood at the back of the room watching Geoffrey hold his hand over her daughter's abdomen. She was in complete shock over the sudden turn of events. She told the healer that her daughter complained of stomach cramps the night before. She thought it was nothing more than that time of the month when she bled. The girl had just reached womanhood two years before, and she'd been expecting some symptoms. But, she didn't think they'd be this severe. She said her daughter was conscious and didn't have a fever when she went to bed, but in the morning, she found the girl soaked with sweat and barely conscious.

The girl's father wasn't in the room. He'd done his duty by getting the healer, and he returned to his fields to harvest the crop as soon as he left. After all, he didn't know anything about womanhood, and like most peasants, he could care less. He had four other children to feed, and if he didn't get the crop in this week, they'd never make it through the winter. The lack of rain was difficult enough, and delaying the harvest by another day could mean the difference between life and death for the family.

Aidan watched his father slowly push on the girl's stomach. He knew he was trying to feel for any swelling that would be caused by an infection. His father closed his eyes as he concentrated, but with each successive touch, he slowly shook his head and moved to a different location. After completing his examination, his father motioned towards the leather bag on the table. Aidan opened the bag and pulled out a canvas pouch that held ten long needles. He took each needle out and held the ends over a candle flame to sear them clean before handing them over.

Geoffrey took the needles and inserted them into her abdomen. He didn't put them in deeply, just enough to stimulate her energy pathways. Aidan saw the mother's concern and smiled in an attempt to calm her. She looked at him with a creased brow, a look he'd seen many times before. It wasn't an easy process to observe, but most times the ending was happy, and the methods of healing were forgotten. Regardless, this was something that had to be done to ensure the disease was properly diagnosed.

Aidan walked to the girl's side and watched his father feel various points around her arms and legs. Geoffrey nodded, and Aidan removed the needles one at a time. When he removed the last needle, the girl moaned, giving Geoffrey the clue he needed. He pressed her inner thigh to make sure. Her weak kidney pulse confirmed his suspicions.

He leaned into Aidan's ear. "She's pregnant," he whispered. Aidan's eyes grew wide.

"She's young," whispered Aidan. He couldn't

believe the girl was pregnant. Peasants often married young, but this girl wasn't married, and they usually waited until they were at least eighteen.

"She's of the age to conceive," whispered his father, careful not to let the mother hear him. He wiped sweat off his brow with a handkerchief he kept in his coat pocket. "Now, I have to find out what's causing this infection." He hadn't felt anything unusual in her abdomen during the examination, but that didn't mean anything, especially if she wasn't far along. He guessed that she was only a few weeks along, and he knew the tiny fetus might be lodged in her tubes. That would cause an infection, so that's where he began.

Geoffrey stood to his feet and looked at the girl's mother. He didn't want to tell her what he'd found yet. He thought it best to wait until he discovered the problem. That way, the mother wouldn't prevent him from treating the girl out of anger. And, if he didn't have to tell her, he wasn't about to. He'd just have to wait and see how it all ended before making that decision.

Aidan immediately knew what his father was up to. The last time they broke the news to a mother, the woman slapped her daughter and left the room. And she wouldn't let the girl come back into her house, forcing her to leave the village in shame. As good as these hard workers were, they had no tolerance for these things.

"I need the amulet," said Geoffrey. Aidan opened the bag and pulled out a long golden chain. Healers usually wore the amulet around their necks, but Geoffrey didn't care much for the attention. Everyone in Heshire knew he was the healer, and that's all that mattered to him. As an instrument, however, it was a powerful healing tool. It was the key instrument of healing for most diseases and could cure most problems if diagnosed correctly. Geoffrey grabbed the round medallion and held it in his hand, staring into the blue stone. This was the healing stone, and it had been passed down generation to generation to each healer in the family.

Geoffrey had yet to teach Aidan how to use the medallion. Aidan figured that he just wasn't ready for that part of his education, and he didn't dare ask his father to teach him. He would when he was ready. Aidan knew how to diagnose a condition, and he knew all of the herbal remedies, but he had to spend time as his father's apprentice before turning to the magic of healing. Healing magic was as old as wizardry, but no one knew who the first healers were, just as they didn't know who the first magicians were. It was all stuff of legend, and legends were of little use to those in the present. It just was, and that's all that mattered.

Healing, just like magic, was an art that was passed down through family lines. You were either born with the gift or you weren't, and no one could aspire to be either. And if you were born into it, you were expected to follow in your parent's footsteps. But who wouldn't want the life? Healer's were well taken care of by the magicians who controlled each shire.

Lord Barton was especially generous to Geoffrey and his family. The people of Heshire were well-loved by the good magician, and he wanted to make sure they were taken care of. He got this attitude from his father and grandfather who had ruled this land since the end of the great war. They were so isolated from the rest of Gornia that they had to be able to take care of themselves. That's why Lord Barton's grandfather took such great pains to ensure that Geoffrey's father moved to the village many years before. At that time, the peasants didn't understand that healers could heal everyone except magician's who were injured by magic. As soon as they understood why he was brought to the village, they were happy to have him there

The girl's mother carefully watched as Geoffrey held the amulet over her daughter's head. She had never seen magic before, and she was excited to be there. Geoffrey glanced her way to make sure she didn't object to magic. Her smile assured him that he could go forward with his plan.

Aidan led the woman away from her daughter. He knew the girl would go into convulsions, and he didn't want her to interfere with the healing process. She moved away, but she wasn't happy about it. Crossing her arms tightly, she watched as Geoffrey invoked the stone's power.

"Hoshok. Pelarium. Riscold. Nelarthum," he said while holding the amulet over the girl. The stone glowed bright blue, and a wave of heat passed over her body as the magic coursed through her energy pathways. At first, only the girl's fingers twitched, but, gradually, her arms and legs began to tremble. Within seconds, the girl went into full convulsions. Aidan had seen this many times. Although he knew nothing of the magic, he knew it worked.

After a few seconds, the girl stopped shaking. Soaked in sweat, she opened her eyes slowly. Her mother dropped to her side and kissed her forehead. She looked at Geoffrey and smiled. "Thank you for bringing my daughter back to me," she said. "I...I don't know how I can ever repay you for this."

Geoffrey didn't acknowledge the mother yet. There was still more to check. He felt the girl's abdomen again. The swelling was gone. "I need to examine her for..." He stopped in mid-sentence.

Aidan knew what he wanted. He reached for the needles and handed them to him. Geoffrey inserted each needle in the same spots as he had before. The mother looked concerned but didn't say a word. At the last energy point, he let out a sigh of relief, looked at Aidan, and nodded his head. The young egg was no longer lodged in her tube, and she showed no signs of being pregnant. While he hated for her to lose the baby, he knew the girl would have died if she hadn't.

Aidan cleaned the needles and put them back in his bag. He was anxious to see how his father handled this situation. The girl needed to know what happened, but the mother didn't.

Geoffrey walked towards the mother and put his arm around her back as he led her towards the door. "Your daughter had an infection. She will be alright."

"Thank you sir," the mother said. Tears ran down her cheeks. "You've saved my little girl."

"No need for any further thanks," said Geoffrey. "But I'd like to talk to your daughter in private if I may." He opened the door and pressed softly on her back. "It will only take a few minutes."

"Is there something wrong?" she asked.

"Nothing's wrong. I just want to talk to her, that's all."

The woman reluctantly walked into the hallway and stared at her daughter as he closed the door.

Aidan wiped the sweat off the girl's forehead when Geoffrey sat at the foot of the bed. He placed his hand on top of her clammy foot. "You've been through a lot," he said. "It'll take some time before you'll regain your strength."

"Yes sir," mumbled the girl. She was weak and tired, and her stomach felt odd, although it didn't hurt anymore.

"I know what happened," Geoffrey said.

The girl looked at him and then closed her eyes in shame.

"It was lodged in your tubes."

She raised her head. "Is it still there?"

"No."

"Does my mother know?"

"No. And I'm not going to tell her." Geoffrey stood. He put his hand on her shoulder. "It's not my place. The next time probably won't end as well."

The girl turned her head and closed her eyes. "It won't happen again." She rolled away from Geoffrey and Aidan and sobbed.

Aidan leaned towards his dad and whispered. "Should we do anything else? Like find out who the father is?"

"It's not our place," he said. "Grab my bag. Our work is done."

Chapter 3

Heshire had been a peaceful village since the war with Sarcus ended. For over one hundred years, villagers had known nothing but the quaint life of a warm southern climate. Most of its citizens farmed the land outside the village walls. Those who didn't farm ran the supply stores that sold everything from fabric to dried grains. There was little need for anything else. Everyone took care of themselves, and those who couldn't were provided food, shelter, and clothing by Lord Barton who followed in the tradition of his father and grandfather after the great war.

The war was a dark time for Heshire. They suffered more than anyone else in Gornia because of their proximity to the border. The main road that connected the two countries ran right through the village, and Sarcugian troops had already burned it to the ground before the Emperor knew that his country was being attacked. Thousands were carted south in shackles and chains. Most of them never returned to their homes again. Those who did escape became the first line of defense, and many of them were slaughtered before the Gornian cavalry arrived from the capital.

Lord Barton's grandfather was the only magician present during that first battle. He was able to hold back the Sarcugian heavy cavalry, but his spells were not enough to counter the council of magicians who approached with the main body.

This council was the ruling body of Sarcus at that time, and they were intent on killing Leopold, Gornia's Emperor, because he dared complain that they were using magic for unjust purposes. He was right. According to the Magician's Code, an ancient manuscript that warned magician's not to use their powers to hurt mortals, the council was in violation. They were caught draining energy from slaves in order to increase their own power, a practice that had been banned for centuries.

Lord Barton's grandfather was injured in that battle and never fully recovered. The magic was too powerful, and no cure was ever found. Even after the treaty had been signed, the Sarcugian magicians would not cure him. It was a sore subject for many years, especially for Lord Barton's father, who never forgave the Sarcugians for what they did. After his father died, he vowed to treat his people well to help ease the pain of their suffering, and he formed his own armed guard that patrolled the border and protected the village.

Lord Barton was relatively young when his father died, and he knew nothing of the horrors the village had endured many years before. His early life was one of peace, and he contemplated reducing the guard many times as a result. However, recently, he had begun to change his mind as rumors started to run rampant about a new threat in Sarcus.

The village had grown from an obscure dot on the map to a small city since the war ended. It was a farming community, but as peace would have it, families got larger and many peasants left their farms in the north and moved to the better climate. It was known throughout the land that Lord Barton treated his subjects better than any other Lord in Gornia.

His manor sat at the north edge of town. Unlike

most rulers, there were no walls. It had been designed to be approachable. Although most people dared not disturb him, if they needed to find him, they could, and that's all that mattered. The village itself had one large street that ran from the front gate to the manor house. Shops, taverns, and even a small restaurant lined the street. Six streets intersected this main road, and that is where the majority of villagers who didn't farm lived.

The entire village was surrounded by a tall wooden wall with walkways where guards could patrol. People could enter and leave the village square through two gates, one on at the south side of the village, and one at the northwest corner. Both gates had been left open since the war, and Lord Barton wasn't even sure the thick doors would close because the huge iron hinges had rusted over the years. There was never a need to close them anyway.

The first sign of trouble began with the odd storm that approached from the south. Guards watched as the purple-black clouds rolled over the mountains on the other side of the Elbe. The rumbling thunder and strange lightning spooked everyone. They'd never seen such an odd storm. Usually, when fronts rolled in, the sky was grey as far as the eye could see. But this storm was dark, and it was only a legion or so in diameter with clear skies all around it.

As rain began to fall on the village, two horsemen rode out of the woods from the road that ran to the Elbe. They carried two shirtless riders who looked soaked to the bone. One of the guards rang the alarm bell as loud as he could.

Upon hearing the alarm, Lord Barton ran outside

towards the south gate where his men had gathered. Villagers and shop keepers ran into the street to see what all of the fuss was about, but the guards ordered them to go back inside. They immediately gathered their families and locked the doors behind them. Braver people looked out the ground floor windows while others peeked from the second floor. This was the first excitement people had experienced in a long time, and they did not want to miss a thing.

The two horses ran through the gate at top speed. Lord Barton's men pulled in front of them and grabbed the reins when the horses slowed. Both riders slumped over the horses' necks and were muttering incoherent statements. Their shirts had been torn off, and their legs were a bloody mess. By the looks of their boots and swords, it was obvious that they were soldiers. The question was, whose soldiers were they? The Emperor had never been to Heshire, so the only person familiar with the Imperial Guard's armor was Lord Barton who had travelled to Tarsus several times. He immediately recognized the seal on their boots, and he ordered his men to bring them to his manor.

Kiro and Rogeris were laid on beds in one of Lord Barton's guest rooms. A female servant pulled the sheets back and opened the drapes so that sunlight could fill the room. Lord Barton excused the guards and servants. He thought he knew where they had come from. He heard the Emperor had sent a delegation into Sarcus, but that was all. These men must have been part of that delegation, he thought.

Kiro was lying in the bed closest to the door. Wincing in pain, he rolled onto his side so that his back wouldn't touch the sheets. Even the faintest breeze caused the wound to burn badly.

Lord Barton examined his back. He'd never seen anything like it before. He sat down on a chair between the two beds. "What's your names?" he asked.

Kiro lifted his head. He was weak and felt very nauseas. The burn felt like it was going deeper inside his body, and that scared him. He coughed, and his eyes rolled back in his head before he passed out, almost falling off the edge of the bed. Lord Barton put his hands on the man's shoulders and pushed him back onto the bed.

He turned around and looked at Rogeris. He looked just as bad, but his eyes were open. Lord Barton stood up and leaned over him.

"What's your name?"

"Rogeris," he mumbled. He reached for the magician. "It hurts."

"I'll get my healer here," said Lord Barton. "Karl!" he shouted.

"Karl!"

"Yes my Lord!" yelled Karl as he jogged down the stairs. "I'm sorry. I was preparing your…"

"Never mind that. I want you to get Geoffrey. Tell him it's an emergency." Lord Barton closed the door sat beside Rogeris. He needed to find out what was going on before Geoffrey got there.

"My healer will be here soon. He will take care of both of you," he assured.

"Thank you," said Rogeris. He leaned onto his left shoulder and grimaced in pain. Sweat rolled down his cheek and landed on the pillow underneath his head. "My Lord, I have an urgent message."

Lord Barton sat straight in the chair and pulled his

cloak out from underneath him, draping it across the back of the chair. He wiped the sweat off the soldier's forehead. "Go ahead, I'm listening."

"We were sent as escort for Lord Nilet. He met Druck at his castle." He winced in pain as he finished the sentence. He lurched back and started to tremble.

Lord Barton laid his hand on Rogeris' thigh. He could feel the magic coursing through the soldier's body, but he didn't dare try to counter the spell until Rogeris told him everything. Rogeris could die in the process, and there was no guarantee that he could suppress the spell. He could tell that this was the result of powerful magic, and he was amazed that they had survived this long. The Healer was their best chance. Perhaps he'd be able to do something to help them.

"Where is Nilet?"

Rogeris looked at Lord Barton through squinted eyes. Everything was getting blurry, and the room began to spin. "Lord Nilet discovered something about Druck. He said we had to get back to Tarsus immediately. We left late in the night thinking we could sneak out, but Druck knew. He cast a spell at Lord Nilet just as we left the castle's gate." His face creased with concern. "I've never seen anything like it. One minute, he was urging us to hurry, and the next, he was slumped over on his horse. We had to strap him to the horse so we could ride."

Lord Barton knew what Druck had done. He'd cast a binding spell on the old magician. It prevented most magicians from using their powers, and it incapacitated them enough so that they could not speak. In essence, he would be in a coma. "Was he coherent?"

"Not really," said Rogeris. He laid back down on his left shoulder and stared at the ceiling. "He was alert when we needed him to be."

"What do you mean?"

"When Druck appeared, he cast a spell. I saw Lord Nilet look towards the south, and I saw his lips move. If it weren't for him, we'd of all been incinerated."

The young magician thought for a minute about what Rogeris had just told him. It was doubtful that a magician as powerful as Druck couldn't have summoned the power to overcome the older magician. Lord Barton stood up and walked toward the window. He looked out onto his courtyard. "What happened after that?"

Rogeris turned as far as he could. "Our horses were incinerated in the blast. Our captain gave us their mounts and told us to find help. They are trapped between the river and the Sarcugians about a quarter of a legion from the river."

Lord Barton turned around. What if this is a trap? If this story isn't true, then he could start a war by sending his men. This was a difficult decision, and he didn't want to be the one to have to make it. "I must know you're telling the truth before I send my men."

"Do what you must. If they get Lord Nilet, Gornia will be in great danger."

"Do you know what Lord Nilet found?"

"No, my Lord. He wouldn't tell us." Rogeris laid back and looked at Kiro. His burn was getting worse and was eating into the muscle. Rogeris could feel the searing heat as well and could only imagine what his back looked like.

Lord Barton rubbed his chin in deep thought. These men might not have much time to spare, and he needed to find out if Rogeris was telling the truth. He'd have to do it before Geoffrey arrived, though. He sat on the bed and placed his hand on the guard's leg. "I'm sorry, but I have to make sure you're telling the truth. I'm going to read your mind, but don't worry, it won't hurt you." He didn't wait for Rogeris to respond. He closed his eyes and allowed his consciousness to flow out of his body. As he hovered over the room, he could see himself sitting on the bed with his hand on the wounded soldier. Rogeris' eyes were wide and his face was tight with fear.

His spirit flowed like a fog into Rogeris' nostrils. Once inside, he could tell what happened in the last few hours of his conscious state. He saw two men riding their horses down a path. They stopped suddenly and Lord Nilet fell. He then saw the approaching clouds. They rode down a steep hill and into a dense thicket. Then they were on a road that led to the river. A bright flash blinded the men. A soldier picked up Lord Nilet and moved him into the thicket. He heard the captain tell Rogeris to get help.

Lord Barton's consciousness poured out of Rogeris' nostrils and flowed back into his body. He immediately stood and ran to the window. "Captain!"

A soldier in brown armor ran into the courtyard. "Yes, my Lord."

"There's no time to explain. Take four men across the river. About a half legion on the road you should find a captain of the Emperor's guard and an old magician. Get them out of there and bring them to me."

The captain was stunned. He'd been to the river

bank many times but had never crossed the river. It was forbidden by the Emperor's edict. Any Gornian caught in Sarcus could be executed. "My Lord?"

"Hurry!" shouted Lord Barton. "You won't be charged. You have my word."

The Captain turned towards his men. In all his years in the Emperor's army and in his last five years in Heshire, he'd never disobeyed an order. "Yes sir."

The guards were dumfounded. None of them wanted to go, and when their captain looked at them, they all stared at the ground. "You heard him! Saddle your horses. We leave in ten minutes!"

Chapter 4

Geoffrey and Aidan returned from the country just in time for dinner. They lived in the same house that Geoffrey grew up in, a gift from Lord Barton's grandfather to his father many years ago. It sat at the back of Lord Barton's courtyard and was the quietest residence in the village.

Aidan had fond memories of this house. To begin with, he was the envy of all of his schoolmates. Living on the Lord's property was a luxury that few could understand. Aidan took it for granted many times until began to understand how others lived. Few people had stone floors, cushy chairs, a library, and a large bedroom of their own. He especially understood his fortune after he became his father's apprentice. The farmers and villagers were freemen, but they lived extremely simple lives.

Annabel was bent over the stove when she heard the two men come in. She had been their servant for over two years. Geoffrey never needed a servant before, but when his wife died, things changed. Lord Barton didn't let a day go by after the funeral before sending Annabel to the house, and she'd been there since. Perhaps it was a gesture of kindness, or perhaps it was because Lord Barton felt guilty for sending the healer to another village when his wife died. It was a day that neither man would forget.

"I'm glad you made it back before dinner," she said. "I don't know how many times I've had to throw away food." She wiped sweat from her brow and reached over to give Aidan a hug. "How are you?"

"It was a tough one," said Aidan. He moved to the stove and looked into the iron kettle. "My favorite! Chicken and vegetable soup." He grabbed the ladle and took a small sip.

"Better watch out," said Geoffrey. "Annabel's going to slap your hand."

Annabel smiled. "I'm getting way too old for that. It's good to see two young men such as yourselves enjoy my cooking."

Geoffrey sat down at the kitchen table, leaned back in the chair, and yawned. "Come to think of it, I'm getting too old for this too."

"Nonsense," said Annabel. She picked up the pot and placed it on the table. "You two want to eat in here or the dining room?"

"Here," said Geoffrey. "The less I have to move, the better."

"Must have been a tough one today," Annabel replied. She opened the oven and pulled out a hot loaf of bread.

"Yea, it was," said Aidan. "This girl…"

"Aidan!" Geoffrey leaned forward. "Remember the first rule of a healer?"

Aidan stopped to think. "Ah, never talk about a patient to anyone."

Geoffrey smiled. His mother always hated that rule. He could remember coming home late many nights, and he couldn't say a word about where he'd been or who he'd seen. It used to infuriate her, but she eventually accepted it.

As the three started eating dinner, there was a knock at the door. "I wonder who in the world that could be," said Annabel. She got up and walked out of the kitchen. Geoffrey and Aidan could still hear her grumble as she opened the door. "Oh, hi there Karl," they heard her say. "What brings you here?"

Karl removed his cap as he walked into the foyer. "I'm sorry to bother you Annabel. Lord Barton needs Master Geoffrey to come to his house immediately."

Annabel closed the door. "Is everything alright with Lord Barton?"

"Oh yes. He's fine," said Karl.

Annabel walked towards the kitchen. "Come in. They're eating dinner right now. Is it something that can wait?"

By the time they got into the kitchen, Geoffrey and Aidan were standing. "What's wrong, Karl?" asked Geoffrey.

"Two soldiers rode into the village an hour ago, and they're badly injured. Lord Barton wants you to tend to them," he said. He looked at the pot of soup on the table. He missed Annabel's cooking. It hadn't been the same since she left the manor. "I'm surprised that you didn't hear the commotion."

"Don't hear too much back here," said Annabel. "Anyway, they just got back in from the country a few minutes ago."

Geoffrey and Aidan headed to the door. Aidan grabbed his father's bag. "You two save us some of that soup and bread, you hear?" He smiled as he shut the door behind him.

They walked as quickly as they could around the rear of the manor towards the servant's side entrance. While they were certainly allowed to go through the front door, Geoffrey always acknowledged his debt to Lord Barton by coming in through the kitchen. He didn't want anyone in the village, including Lord Barton, to think that he was too good for the common folks. Although he wasn't a plebian rank, he wanted people to see him as an equal. It was necessary in order for him to treat them properly. He wished other healers felt the same. Perhaps more people would call them if they didn't prance around like nobles.

One of the maidservants led them to the guest suite where Lord Barton waited. He didn't acknowledge them at first. He didn't even seem to notice when they entered. The maidservant finally cleared her throat to get her master's attention.

The magician spun around with a surprised look on his face. "Oh, there you are Geoffrey," he said. He walked towards the healer and shook his hand. "Pity I don't see you more often. You're a busy man."

"Yes, my Lord," said Geoffrey. "Unfortunately, there's a lot of work to be done."

Lord Barton held his hand out to Aidan. "Your father does a lot of good for our people," he said while shaking the boy's hand. "Learn everything you can from him, and you will be the best healer in all of Gornia."

"Yes sir," Aidan said. He'd always been proud of his father, but there was something special about hearing great things from Lord Barton.

Geoffrey turned to the soldiers. "What happened?"

Lord Barton rubbed his brow. "Anything I tell you must be held in strict confidence," he cautioned.

"Of course," said Geoffrey. "Healers cannot discuss their patients with anyone." He looked at Aidan and nodded. "We will not say a word."

"Good. These men are part of the Emperor's personal guard. They were returning to Tarsus when they were ambushed, and this is how we found them when they arrived."

Geoffrey kneeled beside Kiro and looked at his wounds. His back looked like it had been doused in acid. The skin tissue was completely gone, and part of his muscle was exposed. He sniffed. "Smells like sulfur," he said. He scanned Kiro's legs. The pants were torn and bloodied. "Aidan, I need you to remove his pants," he said. "Much of the blood has dried, so wet them first."

He examined Rogeris next. "Do you know what caused this?"

Lord Barton took a deep breath and looked towards the ceiling. "Only that they were attacked," he said. He knew he shouldn't lie to Geoffrey, but their mission was sensitive. The Emperor would be furious if he told anyone what happened. Even he wasn't supposed to know. And before he was going to say anything, he wanted to talk to Lord Griswold of Sherford. He'd sent a man to him with an urgent message over thirty minutes ago, and he hoped that his friend would arrive before nightfall.

The maidservant brought Aidan a large pitcher of water and a wash basin with a sponge. He squeezed water onto Kiro's legs and peeled the pants off carefully. Most of the cuts were superficial, but there was a large thorn the size of a small branch stuck in his inner thigh. By the looks of it, he was certain that this would require stitching, and he hoped that his father would give him the honor of doing the job.

One of the first things his father taught him was

stitching wounds. He went over the procedure in his head. First, he had to remove the thorn being careful not to break it. Then, he would need to clean the opening with alcohol and water. If the wound was deep, he might have to stitch muscle or veins together with a very fine gut string. A heavier gut string was required to sew together the skin. The last step was probably the most important. He had to smear a thick layer of Silius balm on top of the wound and bandage it immediately, or it would fester and rot.

Geoffrey saw the large thorn sticking out of his thigh and bent over to examine it. "Do you see how it's bleeding?"

Aidan nodded, put his fingers around the thorn, and spread the wound slightly open. More blood poured from the opening. "It's in his vein."

"Get the prong out of my bag and remove the thorn, then cleanse the wound very good. You might have to make the opening larger so you can get to the vein, so have your blade ready."

Aidan's face lit up. This was an excellent opportunity to show Lord Barton that he was a good healer too.

Geoffrey watched as Aidan worked on the wound. He was proud that his son took the job so seriously. He nodded his head in approval and then turned to the burn on Kiro's back.

Lord Barton watched him examine Kiro's back. He quickly glanced at Aidan who had just started to dig into the wound. The sight of blood and that knife sticking through the flap of skin made him feel lightheaded, so he turned back to Geoffrey. He knew the healer would suspect that magic had done this. He tried to figure out how he would answer his questions without giving away too much information.

Geoffrey probed the edges of the skin. He'd never seen anything like this before, and he didn't know where to begin. The skin was slowly evaporating before his eyes, exposing thin layers of fatty tissue and muscle at the edges. The middle of his back was much worse. It had already eaten through the top layer of muscle, exposing small ligaments. The odor bothered him. It was a familiar smell, but he couldn't put a finger on it. He kept thinking about rotten eggs. If he could just remember where he'd smelled it before, perhaps he would have a clue as to how to treat it. He ran his fingers through his hair and sighed. He wondered if he were being told everything.

Chapter 5

Artus held his sword tightly as he looked over the rock. The storm clouds had disappeared over thirty minutes ago, and it was so hot and humid. They needed water soon or they would certainly die of dehydration, he thought. He should have taken his helmet off to catch some of the water when it was raining, although he wasn't certain that magical rain was safe to drink. Even though he'd protected magicians all of his life, he still didn't trust their magic.

There was no sign of the Sarcugians. He'd been listening for them for over an hour, and he hadn't heard a thing. He knew they wouldn't give up their pursuit so easily because it wasn't in their nature to quit. The Sarcugians were known for their fierceness in battle, but they were even more renowned for slaughtering the weak and defenseless. And in their current situation, they would be too good to let go.

Lord Nilet was slumped against the rock and hadn't moved since he grabbed Artus' hand. The old magician looked pale, and his eyes were sinking into his skull. Artus didn't know how much longer he had. Master magicians just didn't succumb to simple spells. It had to be a powerful magic that incapacitated him. That fact bothered Artus more than anything else. If Druck had the ability to do this, what would he do to the rest of Gornia?

A branch cracked in the near distance. Artus sat up and grabbed his sword tightly with both hands. He looked over his right shoulder, but he couldn't see anything through the dense vegetation. The tall oak trees and Partica bushes heavily guarded them behind the stone, but that was a double-edged sword. While they would be difficult to find, it was also be hard to see them, and he didn't like it when he couldn't see his enemy. His heart pounded in his chest, and he had to concentrate as he listened in the distance for anything that might let him know where they were.

Lord Nilet's eyes cracked slightly. He sensed their presence as well. He raised his hand a few inches off his lap and moved his fingers ever so slightly before he blacked out again.

Artus didn't see the magician cast the quick spell. As the Sarcugians closed in, he slowly got to his knees and held his sword toward the noise. He could hear them talking when he saw the first Sarcugian walking through the thicket. Other soldiers trotted down the path on horseback. They were trapped, he thought. This would have to be a fight to the death.

The first Sarcugian soldier came within twenty paces of them, and Artus stood to his feet and faced the man. He was certain that the soldier had seen them. But something was wrong. The hooded swordsman continued to approach without caution. He didn't call for help, and he didn't attack. It was if the two were invisible. Artus was still tense. As the soldier approached, he raised his sword. Just when he was about to strike, Lord Nilet grabbed his foot. The magician looked at Artus and shook his head before passing out again.

Artus forced himself to remain calm. The soldier walked right by them, looked behind the rock, and then he moved toward the road. Lord Nilet had cast some sort of invisibility spell around them, he thought. He shook his head and wiped the sweat from his brow. "A little magic, eh? You came through for us, my Lord," he whispered.   The Sarcugians scoured the dense forest for another hour. Several soldiers walked within a few feet of their position, and none of them detected anything unusual. A horseman rode off the path and stopped in front of them to bark orders at the rest of the soldiers. He thought they had been discovered when the horseman sniffed the air and looked right at him. After a few long seconds, the officer shook his head and rode back to the road. A few minutes later, the soldiers headed north towards the mountain.

Druck looked deeply into the crystal on top of his staff. He knew the two men were down there, but he couldn't see them. His face wrinkled with anger when the captain returned with his men.

"Lord Druck, we cannot locate them. They've disappeared."

Druck's lip began to quiver. "They're down there! What do you mean you cannot find them?!"

"My Lord, we've covered every inch of the road and forest to the river, and they're not there."

Druck knew that Nilet had cast a shadow spell. He just didn't think the magician had enough power left to do so. Even he couldn't see them through his crystal, and that meant the old man was still strong. "Never mind," he told the captain. "He's bound in my spell and won't be able to recover. He doesn't have much time."

The captain was relieved that Druck didn't punish him. His face relaxed as he leaned over in the saddle. "Can he be cured?"

Druck smiled and turned to the captain. "No." He pulled the hood of his cloak over his head and spun around. A strong gust of wind blew, and he disappeared leaving the captain and his men to return home on their own.

Artus waited thirty minutes before getting back on his feet. He cautiously walked toward the road, careful not to make any noise. He kneeled at a bush and peered cautiously towards the mountain. Druck and his men had left, it seemed, but he wasn't about to go into the road in case they had laid a trap for them.

He was closer to the river than he thought. He was no more than a hundred paces from the bank, and if help didn't arrive soon, he would have to carry Lord Nilet across. It was a shallow river and wasn't very wide, so it was possible.

As he walked back to the rock, a sharp pain in his stomach bent him over. Falling to the ground, he looked down and saw that the hole in the breastplate had gotten much bigger, and his skin was burned, leaving the muscle exposed. He took his handkerchief and placed it over the wound. The pain was so intense that he got dizzy, but he refused to pass out. He got to his feet and stumbled back to Lord Nilet.

By the time Artus heard the horses splash through the river, it was getting dark. He was sure this wasn't the Sarcugians because they wouldn't have made so much noise. Perhaps they were the rescue party he'd sent Kiro and Rogeris after. He'd been wondering about his two men, praying that they made it to Heshire. The longer they were out there alone, the more he had convinced himself that they didn't make it.

He moved quietly towards the road and leaned around a thick oak to get a view of the road. Five horsemen wearing brown leather armor trotted cautiously up the road with swords drawn. He waited until they passed, looking carefully at their breastplates. Once he saw Lord Barton's eagle crest, he was certain they were there to get them.

Leaning against the tree, he took a step towards the road. The pain in his stomach returned, and he buckled over and fell, dropping his sword to the ground.

The Heshire guards heard the sword as it fell into the stony soil, and they turned quickly in their saddles to find Artus lying limp beside his weapon. "That's him," said the Captain. He rode towards Artus and ordered his men to dismount.

Artus grabbed the soldiers' arms and picked himself off the ground. Everything was fuzzy, and his head was spinning in circles. "Heshire?"

"We were sent to bring you back to Lord Barton's manor," said the captain. "Where is Lord Nilet?"

Artus raised his arm and pointed into the woods. "Behind the boulder." He collapsed and fell to the ground.

"Put him on your horse," the captain told one of

his men. He pointed at the other three. "Get Lord Nilet. We need to get out of here as soon as we can."

The men ran into the woods. They wanted to get across the river quickly because this was a bad place to be. They found the old magician exactly where Artus told them he'd be. One of the men picked him up and slung him across his shoulder and walked back to the road. As soon as they got the two on their horses, they galloped across the river and headed back to Heshire.

Chapter 6

Lord Griswold rode into Heshire an hour before dusk. He hurried to get there as quickly as he could as soon as he'd received the urgent message from Lord Barton. The two had become friends since he took possession of Sherford. Although they'd only known each other for a year, they became close after realizing how much they had in common. Their lands were close, and they were isolated from the rest of Gornia, so they learned to consult with each other before making any major decisions. As well, they were young, handsome, single men. In addition, neither one had been a magician for that long. Lord Barton barely finished his apprenticeship before his father died, and Lord Griswold finished his right before coming to Sherford.

Sherford, like Heshire, bordered Sarcus about fifty legions west of Lord Barton's shire. It was a rocky, hilly land ideally suited for grape-growing, and most of his peasants were in the wine trade in one way or another. Unlike Lord Barton, Lord Griswold inherited a feudal system that could trace its history for over a thousand years. He was more feared than loved, and he barely made a visit to the countryside unless it was to arrest someone for not paying taxes. He kept a fairly large armed unit in the village to control his people rather than protect them. Lord Barton didn't care for the way his friend ran his shire, but that was none of his business, so he left it at that.

Lord Griswold hurried inside the house looking for Lord Barton. A head peeked out of the kitchen.

"There you are, my Lord," said the maidservant. She hurried into the waiting room, wiping her hands on her apron. "Lord Barton is waiting for you." She pointed down the hall. "Right this way."

As soon as they reached the bedroom door, Lord Griswold burst in, nearly knocking Aidan to his knees. He didn't bother to look at the young man nor did he apologize. "I got here as soon as I received your message," he said as he stepped around the bed to shake Lord Barton's hand. "Good to see you again." He didn't acknowledge the two soldiers or Geoffrey. Anyone other than a magician was inconsequential to him.

"Good to see you," said Lord Barton. "Let's go to my library. We need to talk, and my healer has work." Lord Griswold didn't take much stock in healers. He never had, and he wasn't afraid to say as much. Since their powers could do little for magicians, he didn't have any respect for them.

As soon as they entered the library, Lord Barton shut the door and locked it.

"What's the hurry?" asked Lord Griswold. "I just got here. What about a drink first?"

Lord Barton plopped down in one of the reading chairs by the window and buried his face in his hands. "There's no time."

"Time for what?" He sat down. "There's always time for a drink, especially after a long ride."

"Not today." Lord Barton stood and walked to the window, staring blankly at the fountain in the courtyard. "We've got a problem, and I don't know what to do."

Lord Griswold stood. "What kind of problem?" He walked to the other window and looked out.

"Druck."

Lord Griswold turned to face his friend. "Druck?" He slung his cloak over his right shoulder and sat in the desk chair. "How have we got a problem with Druck? Isn't he still busy with Parthage?"

Parthage was a small country that sat on the southern border of Sarcus. Druck invaded it five years earlier, and the rumor was that he was stretched to his limit.

Lord Barton scratched his head. "You're right. Everything I've heard points to the fact that he's bogged down there, but he's up to something, and I don't like it."

"How do you know he's up to something?"

"Because two of the Emperor's personal guard rode into the village today. They are in that bedroom right now fighting for their lives."

Lord Griswold rose to his feet and walked back to the window. "Perhaps they were ambushed. It happens, you know?"

Lord Barton slammed his fist on the window ledge. "They came from Sarcus! One of them told me that Lord Nilet was with them. He said they were on a mission for Leopold. They were chased by Druck's guard all the way to the Elbe!"

Lord Griswold leaned against the window and closed his eyes. He had heard stories of Lord Nilet's great magical powers since he was a boy. The master magician was the Emperor's right-hand man, and if he were in Sarcus, there must have been a good reason for the trip.

Lord Barton turned to face his friend. "He told me that Lord Nilet was struck by some magical spell that incapacitated him." He paused. "He's in a coma, and he's trapped across the river with the captain of their detachment.

"And the injuries to those men?"

"Magic. An incineration spell, I suppose."

"It should have killed them," said Lord Griswold. "Druck is a very powerful magician."

"Lord Nilet must have done something. I'm not sure." He brushed his sweat-soaked hair out of his eyes.

Lord Griswold walked to the bookshelf and pulled out a book. He thumbed through the pages to give him something to do while he thought. "Have you sent your men after them?"

"Of course I did. Five rode out a couple of hours ago."

"And?"

"They haven't returned yet."

Lord Griswold pulled his cloak away from his neck. "Are you certain this isn't a trick?"

"I already thought about that. I read one of the soldier's minds. Everything he said was true."

Lord Griswold smiled. "Nice. You're going to be a good magician yet."

"I didn't have a choice. This isn't a game!"

"I'm sorry. I didn't mean anything by it."

Lord Barton poured a glass of brandy for each of them. "I'm kind of in the middle of all of this, and I don't know what to do."

"Let's see if your men find anyone before we jump to conclusions." He took a sip of brandy as they sat in silence and watched the sun set in the distance.

Aidan sewed the wound and applied the healing salve before bandaging it. He seared the needle over a flame before putting it back in the bag. "How are you doing over there?"

Geoffrey pulled at the edge of Kiro's skin with his probe and watched as it disintegrated. "I don't know what's going on here, but I suspect it has something to do with magic."

Aidan leaned over his father to get a better look. "Can you heal him? I thought we could cure anyone who'd been injured by a spell as long as they weren't a magician?"

Geoffrey grabbed the headboard and stood. "Remember rule two of healing. You can't cure it if you can't diagnose it." He shook his head. "If I don't know what I'm dealing with, I can't help him."

"What about the medallion? Can it cure them without a specific diagnosis?"

Geoffrey shook his head. "The diagnosis is the key." He patted Aidan's shoulder. "I know I haven't taught you everything yet. The incantation is specific to the cure, and you can't determine the incantation unless you know the cure."

Aidan was eager to begin the magical portion of his training. He felt like he was ready, but his father obviously didn't. More questions, he thought. Perhaps if I ask enough questions, he'll realize I'm ready to learn. "How come you can't guess the problem and say the incantation?"

Geoffrey was impressed with his son's question. "If

you guess wrong, it will kill the patient."

Aidan's heart sank. He never realized the power of the healer. He couldn't imagine that one mistake could kill a person, yet it made sense. This was something his father never talked about.

Geoffrey looked at the wound. He could see the faint glimpse of Kiro's lower vertebrae, and he knew that the soldier wouldn't make it unless something was done quickly. "Our world is a world of magic and knowledge. The early magicians made sure that healers weren't as powerful as them. They gave us enough magic to be useful but that's about it. It takes a long time to become a master healer. You have to know how to diagnose and how to treat. We have to be intelligent and magical." He chuckled. "They only have to be magical."

Aidan poured a glass of water for his father. He knew these cases were difficult for him. "You need to drink." He paused to think of the ramifications of his next comment. "Perhaps Lord Barton could give you some insight."

Geoffrey put the glass on the table and nodded his head. "That's exactly what I was thinking. They don't have much time." He walked out of the room in a hurry.

One of the guards started shouting in the courtyard. Lord Barton jumped out of his chair, spilling his brandy on the rug. He ran to the window. "Are they back?"

"Yes, my Lord, they just rode through the village

gate."

Before he had finished his sentence, five horse-men galloped into the courtyard. Lord Barton rushed towards the door. "Save the drink for later," he told Lord Griswold. "My men are back!"

He threw open the door and ran into the hallway, bumping into Geoffrey on his way out.

"My Lord, I was just about..."

Lord Barton didn't look back. "Not right now!"

Lord Griswold walked out of the room looking quite full of himself. His arrogance annoyed Geoffrey. "Fool," Geoffrey mumbled.

Lord Barton ran to his captain, grabbing the reins of his horse as the soldier dismounted. "Are they alright?" he asked. Before the captain could answer, he dashed behind the horse and saw Lord Nilet slung over another horse.

"Alive, I hope," said Lord Griswold.

Lord Barton listened to the old magician's chest. "He's breathing!" He looked around at the other horses. He didn't see the captain of the detachment. "There was another man. Did you find him?"

"Yes, my Lord," said the captain. "But..."

"But what?!" demanded Lord Barton.

One of the horsemen dismounted and bowed his head. "I'm sorry, my Lord. I had him secure on my horse. We crossed the river and rode. The next thing I knew, he was gone."

"Gone?! What do you mean gone?!"

"My Lord, he just disappeared," answered the captain. "We doubled back, but the only thing we found was his clothes." He held up Artus' breastplate as evidence.

Lord Griswold looked at the large hole that had been burned in the breastplate. He leaned into Lord Barton's ear. "Druck's work," he whispered.

Lord Barton looked at Artus' armor. "He must have had a mortal wound."

"In the stomach," said Lord Griswold. "It would have killed him quicker than the two inside."

Lord Barton cradled the old man in his arms. He walked carefully up the steps past Geoffrey. "Karl!" he yelled.

Karl stuck ran to the front door as soon as he saw Lord Barton. "Yes, my Lord."

"I am putting him in my chambers. See to it that no one enters the room except me and Lord Griswold."

"Yes sir."

Geoffrey followed the two magicians into the house but stayed behind with Karl as they walked upstairs. "He doesn't want me to examine him?"

Karl put his hand on Geoffrey's shoulder. "I'm afraid not."

Geoffrey walked slowly down the hall. All of this commotion, all of this magic…it just didn't make sense. Nothing like this had ever happened in Heshire before, at least in his lifetime. He knew something was going on, and he needed to find out before more people died.

Aidan was staring blankly at Kiro's back when his father walked in. "I saw everything through the window," he said. "What's going on?"

Geoffrey shook his head. "I don't know, but I don't like it. Something's terribly wrong."

"What can I do to help?" asked Aidan.

"Get some rest," Geoffrey said. "I've got a lot to think about."

After another thirty minutes, the edges of Kiro's skin started to glow, making it look like he'd caught on fire. It didn't take more than ten seconds before his entire body was eaten away, leaving nothing but his undergarments on the bed.

Geoffrey jumped out of his chair and walked behind Rogeris' bed. His flesh was glowing too, and within a few seconds, his body disappeared.

Aidan had been napping on the floor in the corner of the room when he heard his father get up. By the time he looked up, both soldiers were gone. "Where did they go?" he asked. It was magic," said his father, and he slammed his fist into the bed.

Aidan had never seen Geoffrey get angry before. He looked at the empty beds. "Just like that?"

"Just like that," mumbled his father. "They never had a chance because no one would tell me anything!" He yelled loudly, hoping that Lord Barton could hear him. Taking a deep breath, he calmed himself. "Pack the bag. We're done."

"What about the man they just brought in?"

"If we're called, we'll come back. Right now, I could use some food and a little sleep." He walked out. It was dark outside now, and there was an unusually cold wind blowing from the south.

Chapter 7

Geoffrey and Aidan returned home at a little past nine that evening. Their day had begun at first sunlight and had just ended. Many times, this was a normal day for a healer. Sometimes, they wouldn't come home at all, choosing to sleep in someone's house until they rode at first sunlight. Years of this life were wearing on Geoffrey. His once brown hair was now full of grey, and his eyes were boxed in with heavy creases.

Aidan had noticed his father's moods lately. Just last week, after he went to bed, he heard his father sobbing in the library. Sneaking downstairs, he peeked through the door and saw his dad sitting in from of a portrait of his mother. He wanted to comfort him, but Annabel pulled him away explaining that his father needed "his" time to grieve. Certainly, Aidan had grieved, but as time went on, he had come to terms with her death. His father, though, spent most of the first year angry that he wasn't there to save her. Now, he supposed, he was dealing with the guilt.

His mother's death was a huge blow to the whole village. It was never easy when a wife and mother died, but when it was the Healer's wife, it became a tragedy that people would remember for years. When Lord Barton asked them to go to Sherford to help Lord Griswold's uncle, his wife was as healthy as she'd ever been. It was a three-hour ride to Sherford, and they had been with the old man for another five hours. On their way back home, they met Karl on the road, and that's where they got the news.

It was a total shock to the two. When they got

back home, they found her lying in bed. Lord Barton had been with her when she died. He explained that she collapsed in the garden early in the afternoon, and she died about an hour later. He'd sent Karl to get them, but it was too late to save her. Geoffrey deduced that she had a bad heart, but there was no true way to find out unless he cut her, and he would not do that to his wife. Ever since, he had blamed himself for not discovering her ailment before it was too late.

Since that day, Geoffrey worked longer than usual and spent more time with his patients. And anytime someone died while under his care, he took it harder than he used to. The loss of the two soldiers was no different. When he walked into the house, he went directly to his library and sat alone in thought with a large glass of wine.

Aidan went to the kitchen, leaving his father to his thoughts. Annabel left soup in the kettle, and Aidan pulled a bowl out of the cupboard and sat down to eat. When he took his first bite, Annabel walked in and put her hands on his shoulders.

Aidan knew she was coming. He could smell the cinnamon spice of her sweet perfume before she opened the door. She wasn't his mother, but she was a close second as far as he could tell.

"Bad night?" she asked as she rubbed his shoulders with her wrinkled hands.

"Yea," he said as he ate his soup. He put the spoon down and leaned back. "How could you tell?"

"I may be old, but I'm not blind." She sat down in a chair beside him and stirred his soup. "Your father's taking it hard."

Aidan shook his head. "It's that obvious?"

"Boy, I know you two good enough to know how your day's gone." Aidan was the son she never had. She worked too much to ever marry, and when she came to the healer's house after his wife died, she became much more than their servant. She became a member of their family, a role she loved to have.

Aidan smiled and took another sip of soup. "It was the worst thing I've ever seen, and Dad said the same." He shook his head and placed both elbows on the table. "I don't know if I'm cut out for this."

Annabel pointed at him with her bony finger. "I don't want to hear you talk like that anymore! You're a healer. That's all there is to it. It's been determined by your birth and your training. Giving up on healing is like a magician not casting a spell. It's unheard of!"

Aidan shook his head. "What's your problem?" he asked. "I'm just a little down right now, that's all."

She looked into his eyes. "My problem is you're questioning your ability to heal when thousands of people will be counting on YOU to take care of them and their families."

Aidan shook. "I'm not going to quit, Annabel. I'm just a little upset right now, that's all."

"What's your father always say about 'feelings?'" she asked.

"Rule number three...leave your emotions at the door."

"Listen to your father."

Aidan pushed the bowl to the center of the table. "Sometimes I wish he'd follow his own rules."

Annabel hugged him. "It's been tough on your father since your mother died. He's placed a big burden on his shoulders, and he's the only person who can remove it." She patted his back. "Now for you mister, eat your soup. I'll get you a nice cup of cool milk to go with it."

Lord Barton stood over the old magician. He hadn't moved since he'd laid him in the bed. His eyes didn't open, his mouth stayed closed, and his arms and legs were limp. The only sign of life was his breathing, and it was shallow.

"It took a powerful spell to do this," said Lord Barton as he pulled the heavy comforter over Lord Nilet's chest. He knew Lord Nilet's reputation. Old magicians were rarely affected by another magician's magic, especially a younger magician like Druck. Something just didn't add up.

Lord Griswold sat on the thick-cushioned couch in front of the fireplace. "I'm going to have to get one of these," he said as he rubbed the couch's heavy silk fabric.

Lord Barton threw his hands in the air, keeping his back turned to his friend. "Aren't there more important things to discuss?" he asked.

"What could be more important than fine furniture?" asked the pompous Griswold. He chuckled. "What do you want me to say?"

"I brought you here to discuss matters of great importance, not how to furnish your manor."

Lord Griswold walked to the window and pulled back the satin drapes. The village was very quiet. The only people outside at this hour were the guards who patrolled the perimeter at the top of the wall. Lord

Barton had doubled the guard this evening and was even considering bringing more soldiers to the village as a precaution. "We can discuss this problem all night and never reach a conclusion."

Lord Barton walked toward his friend, grabbed his shoulder, and turned him from the window. "What do you mean by that? We have no power over this situation?"

Lord Griswold smiled and brushed his long brown hair over his head. "We're over our heads. You know we can't help him. I mean, if he couldn't help himself, who are we to try?"

"Something must be done!"

Lord Griswold bit his lip and nodded. "Yes, I agree. Something must be done."

"What can we do? Do you have a solution?" Lord Barton was getting tired of this cat and mouse game. While he accepted his eccentric behaviors, he was not very fond of his attitude.

"It's really quite simple. One of us should go to Tarsus and speak to the Emperor."

"Are you volunteering?" Lord Barton knew the answer already, but asked the question anyway.

Lord Griswold smiled and clasped his hands together. "Why, I would be honored to go. Thank you for asking." He never needed a reason to go to the city. Unlike Lord Barton who had been raised in the south, he resented being stuck in the country so far from civilization. He especially wouldn't want to miss an opportunity to meet with the Emperor.

Lord Barton rolled his eyes. He knew the reason he wanted to go. It certainly wasn't for love of country. But, since he needed to protect Heshire, he couldn't go, so sending Griswold was the only option he could consider. He pointed to Lord Nilet. "He stays here, though. I'm not sure he'd make it, and he'd slow you too much."

Lord Griswold grabbed his gloves. "I'll leave right now. I'll never get any sleep tonight anyway, so I might as well ride through."

"I am sure you'll rest tomorrow."

"Certainly. I should be about half-way there by then. You know that nice inn at Werth?"

"Yes." He knew of it, but he'd never stayed there.

"That's where I'll be tomorrow night. Then, I'll ride until I get to Tarsus. I hope to see the Emperor in two days."

"Hurry back with an answer."

Lord Griswold extended his hand. "I certainly will."

Lord Barton didn't believe he'd try to hurry at all. He didn't take this situation seriously enough. He wished that he could transport to Tarsus, but most magicians didn't have that sort of power. To his knowledge, only a few master magicians in the history of the world have ever been able to do something like that.

Geoffrey sipped on his second glass of wine as he thought about the day. He knew he had a problem with death. That was a demon that he'd live with for the rest of his life. It was different when people died after he'd done everything he could for them. After all, he was a healer not a god. He couldn't raise the dead or bring back the dying. There was only so much a healer could do. Most of the time, a cure could be found, but there was the time for death, and everyone, even healers and magicians, had to face that certainty.

What bothered him most, however, was when someone died, and he couldn't help them, and that is what happened with the two soldiers. Had Lord Barton shared some information, he could have possibly helped them, or at least eased their pain. But the usually benevolent Lord was oddly quiet and mysterious about the whole matter, and Geoffrey knew enough about people to know when they were either lying or holding back information. Healers had to have that instinct to get to the bottom of a matter, especially when it came to country folks who had an innate ability to keep relevant details about their lives secret.

Aidan poked his head around the door. His talk with Annabel energized him, and he thought he'd share a little of that energy with his father. "You busy?" he asked.

He startled his father, causing him to spill a little wine on his shirt. "No," he said as he wiped the wine off with his hand. "Come on in."

Aidan sat on the couch and laid back. "I can't sleep."

"Did you eat?"

"Yes. Annabel left soup for you. She says you need to eat before you go to bed."

Geoffrey smiled. "She does, does she?" He took another gulp of his wine. "I'm just thinking about those two men."

"What about?"

"Remember how I've told you to leave your emotions at the door?"

Aidan chuckled. He'd heard this speech just a few minutes ago. "Yes, I remember it."

"Well, I'm having a difficult time doing that right now."

Aidan leaned forward. This was the first time that his father ever opened up to him about emotions. "What are you having a hard time with?"

Geoffrey stood and walked to the fireplace. He wasn't sure if he should discuss his concerns with Aidan, but he had no one else to talk to, and he needed to get it off his chest. "You know, healing is like a fight. You have to know your opponent before you face him." He picked up the stoker and drew imaginary circles in the air with it. "If you know who you're dealing with, you can come up with a way to beat him. If you don't know him, you'll lose every time."

Aidan knew exactly what his father meant, but he wanted to tell his father that he shouldn't take it too hard. "Sometimes it's impossible to know your opponent, though, and you have to accept defeat when it's handed to you."

Geoffrey hung the poker back on the fireplace. "I understand that, but when a friend knows something that will help you, and he refuses to tell you, it makes defeat hard to accept."

Aidan stood. "Do you really think Lord Barton withheld information that could have saved those men's lives?"

"I told you he was. He's a magician. If anyone could discover what sort of spell had been cast, it was him. And he didn't say a word." He slammed his fist against the hearth. "If I had known what magic I was dealing with, I am certain that I could have stopped it!

There's no magic out there that can't be cured by the healing stone!"

"Maybe there's something going on that we don't know about. They found that old man and brought him in. Think that has something to do with it?"

"Of course it does." He paced back and forth. "And that lord from Sherford..." He paused and looked at the floor. "What's his name?"

"Lord Osgood's nephew?"

"Yes."

"Griswold, I think."

Geoffrey continued to pace. "Yes, that's it. What is he doing in Heshire? He hasn't been here in months."

"But I think Lord Barton's fairly close to him," said Aidan.

"His timing is impeccable." Geoffrey stopped and rubbed his chin. "No, something's not right. It feels..."

"Feels like what?"

Geoffrey turned to Aidan. "Like black magic."

Aidan's eyes grew wide. "Black magic? What makes you think that?" Black magic had been banned since the great war. No magician in Gornia would ever step over the line to dabble in the black arts because the penalty was immediate death. Magicians wouldn't even experiment with it because black magic so obviously changed their appearance that they would be recognized the moment they stood in front of another magician. It was one of the first things apprentices learned.

"That spell...the one that killed those two men... it had to be black magic. It just makes sense. It's why Lord Barton couldn't help them...why he was so silent about the whole thing…it's why he wouldn't let me near that man."

"But if that's true, then who did it?"

"Druck."

"If what you say is true, then someone has to warn the Emperor. Black magic is banned in Sarcus too, and if someone is breaking the treaty, then it could mean another war."

"Or it could mean they have declared war on us already." Geoffrey returned to his chair and grabbed his glass of wine. "You were too young to remember your grandfather. He told many stories about the Sarcugian invasion, and none of them had a happy ending."

"I've read about it in my books," said Aidan.

"History books don't do it justice," said his father. "No one alive knows the horrors our grandparents experienced. And it was all because of black magic."

Aidan had never heard anything about black magic other than from his history books. The subject was taboo for the most part, and anyone who asked questions about it was viewed as suspect. "What would they want with us?"

"They want the magicians. They're the ones with the true power. They take them hostage, drain their power, and leave them to die. Then they come for the healers. We have powers they don't possess, and they want to take it from us. Once they've done that, they go for everyone else."

"How can they use people who have no powers?"

"They take their life energy. It gives them strength. During the war, their council only went after magicians. They let their army take everyone else prisoner and held them until they had defeated as many magicians as possible. Then they started the great slaughter."

Aidan tried to remember his history, but he read the stories too long ago to remember much. "How did we defeat them?"

"Magicians in the north were fairly protected from the war. Because most of the war was fought in the south. It took time, but the Emperor convinced them to take a stand, and they were finally able to defeat the council. Our army did the rest."

"Are you afraid the same thing is happening again?"

"It's starting to add up."

"So what do we do?"

"I don't have a clue."

Lord Barton sat beside the bed and felt Lord Nilet's head. "What am I supposed to do?!" he asked. "You came here for a reason, and I don't know why!" He leaned back in the chair. "And you can't tell me!"

He threw his cloak over his shoulder stood. "I've tried everything! Nothing works!"

Lord Nilet remained motionless. There was every indication that he was at death's door, but were that the case, his powers would be diminished. But they weren't, and that was a fact that Lord Barton knew too well.

That left only two possibilities. Either Druck's powers were so great that he overcame the master magician, or Lord Nilet cast a spell over himself that protected him and the information he had from Druck.

Druck certainly had enough power to defeat most magicians in Gornia. After all, he practiced black magic – he was certain of that by the wounds he saw on the soldiers. He guessed it was possible that black magic could overcome an experienced magician. There were spells he'd never heard of in the black arts, and he was sure Lord Nilet wasn't protected from them all.

As for the other possibility, had Lord Nilet cast a spell on himself that would have incapacitated him, he would have left himself the ability to come out of it – a trapdoor. If that were the case, why hadn't he regained consciousness by now?

Lord Barton's thoughts raced back and forth until he couldn't take it anymore. And then he started feeling sorry for himself. He wasn't fit to deal with all of this, he thought. He had only been a magician for a few years, and he still didn't have complete control over his powers. Not that he'd been practicing much lately. Leading a shire was more work than one could imagine, especially as far away from the capital as Heshire was.

He wished he had listened to his father when he told him to read the *Book of Magic* every day and "practice, practice, practice until you've mastered every spell." But he had no desire to be a master magician, so he didn't practice, and he hadn't read the book in months.

He was happy to have his minor magic – casting a shield around his body to keep himself from getting wet in the rain, making fireballs when he needed to get warm, keeping his wine from spoiling – things like that. Everything else, he left to nature. He was sure the farmers wanted him to make rain more often, but he didn't. Not because he couldn't do it, but because it tampered with the natural order, and he didn't want to spend his life making rain, stopping floods, calming earthquakes, and slowing winds. Once magic was used for these extra-natural things, it changed everything, and he'd heard stories about other magicians that blew his mind. And they were practicing legal magic!

Now that Lord Nilet had arrived, however, his entire outlook on magic had changed. Facing a threat as ominous as Druck required a powerful magician with experience. For the first time, Lord Barton wished he were that person, but deep down, he knew the man for that job was now lying unconscious in his bed. He wasn't even sure that the young Emperor, Leopold III, was up to the task.

Chapter 8

Annabel had waited an hour later to cook breakfast since they'd had a long day the day before, and she wanted them to sleep. Her mind was set on lifting their spirits any way she could, so she decided to make their favorite meal of bacon, eggs, and toasted bread. There was no better way of waking up, she reasoned, than with the smell of frying bacon. That should get them started on the right foot.

As she put the first few strips of fresh bacon on the skillet, someone knocked softly on the front door. "I can't believe it," she mumbled. "Of all the times." She took the skillet off the oven and slid it onto the table. The knocking continued. "I'm coming, I'm coming," she griped. "You don't have to be so impatient." She wiped her hands on her apron and opened the door. "What's the hurry?"

Lord Barton was leaning against the wall.

"My Lord," she said. Her face was red. "I..I didn't think…"

"No need to…apologize," he said.

"Please come in," she said. "Master Geoffrey isn't awake. He had a very long day, and I decided to let him sleep."

Lord Barton stumbled into the room. His breath reeked of liquor, and his eyes were glazed. Annabel had never seen him get this way before, even when his father died. He staggered towards the stairs and fell face first. She ran over to him and helped him up. "Thank you, Annabel," he said. "He raised his finger and shook it at her. "Smells like bacon. You know that's my favorite."

"Yes, my Lord, I remember," she said.

"Might I stay and have some?"

"Yes, my Lord. I would love to..."

He stood and stumbled towards the kitchen before finding his balance against the wall. "I'll wait until it's ready. No hurry." He rolled off the wall and landed hard on the floor.

"My goodness!" cried Annabel. She ran up the stairs and pounded on Geoffrey's door. "Master Geoffrey! Master Geoffrey!"

Geoffrey opened the door quickly. He hadn't fallen asleep until very early in the morning, and his head ached, and his body felt limp from exhaustion. "What's the problem?" he grumbled.

"It's Lord Barton! He knocked on the door, he fell in the kitchen...I think he's drunk!"

"I'll be down in a second." He shut the door put his clothes on. Lord Barton hadn't been to the house since his wife's funeral, and he'd never seen him drunk.

Aidan ran out too. He'd heard the commotion and started dressing as soon as he heard Annabel. He got to the kitchen before his father, rolled Lord Barton over, and checked to make sure he was breathing. He then leaned over and smelled the magician's breathe.

"Get away from him!" ordered his father.

Aidan's face turned pale. His father had never yelled at him before. He couldn't understand what he'd done wrong. "All I did was check..."

"It could be magic!" He stood over Lord Barton with his amulet. "If it's black magic, it could transfer to you through contact."

64

Annabel felt light-headed. She'd never heard anything like this before. She wished the world would be rid of all this magic. It would make things much simpler.

Aidan stood up. "But it's not black magic. It's not magic at all unless liquor is considered magic."

Geoffrey was stunned. He lowered the amulet. "Are you certain?"

"Smell his breath. He's drunk."

Geoffrey knelt down. Aidan was right. He could smell the alcohol. All those thoughts of black magic the night before had affected his judgment. "You're right, son. He's drunk." He stood and placed the amulet around his neck. It was the first time he'd worn it in years. "Let's get him to the library. We've got to sober him up."

Aidan grabbed Lord Barton's shoulders while his father got his legs. They picked him up and carried him to the couch. Annabel brought a blanket and placed it over his legs before taking his boots off. "Where's his cloak?" she wondered.

Aidan pulled the blanket back. "Where IS his cloak?" He never went anywhere without it.

The fabric of the cloak itself was made by the magic of the magician's teacher. In Lord Barton's case, his father made it as a gift when he finished his apprenticeship. That only added sentimental value, though. The true power was in each fiber of the fabric. The entire body of magical knowledge that his father had, as well as those of his ancestors, were contained in the fibers. When he used his magic, he would use the full power of his ancestral line. Magician's who came from powerful ancestral traditions began with more power than those who came from weaker traditions. This was how the hierarchy of magicians was determined.

"Do you think it was taken while he was drinking?" asked Annabel.

"Impossible," said Geoffrey. A magician's cloak can never be removed by anyone other than the magician. The clasp is locked with magic."

"That's odd," said Aidan.

"What's odd?" asked his father.

"After we talked about the war last night, I pulled out one of my old books and started reading it. It said the council defeated many weaker magicians by taking their cloaks."

"Black magic, magical cloaks, healing stones – all of this is giving me a headache," exclaimed Annabel. "I'm going to the kitchen to finish breakfast if that's alright with you." She left before either of them could say a word.

"Remember my bacon," slurred Lord Barton.

"My Lord, you're awake," said Geoffrey.

"Yes, yes...I just fell to sleep for a moment." He sat up and swayed on the couch. "I've drunk too much, I'm afraid."

"Sleep it off here, my Lord, if that's suitable to you. There's no need..."

"Three things before I do, Geoffrey."

"Yes, my Lord."

"First, make sure she saves me some bacon."

"Of course, my Lord."

"And second, my cloak is hanging in my room. I don't wear it to bed, you know."

"Of course not, my Lord."

"Third, remind me when I wake that I have something very important to discuss with you." He lied down, pulled the blanket over his shoulders, and rolled onto his side.

Chapter 9

Lord Barton woke in the middle of the afternoon. His head pounded with every heart beat, he was dizzy, and he wanted to vomit. Anything to make him feel better, but the only thing he had in his empty stomach was acid, and it burned his throat badly. As soon as he pushed himself into a sitting position, he looked around the library. He barely remembered coming to Geoffrey's house that morning. At least he didn't wake up in some strange woman's bed, he thought.

A basin of fresh water and a cloth were lying on the table next to the couch. He dipped the cloth in the water, wiped his face off, and splashed his head. The cool water calmed the pounding and cleared his head of fogginess. He stood slowly, walked over to the bookcase, and casually scanned Geoffrey's collection as he gathered himself.

"You're finally awake, my Lord."

He turned towards the door. It was Annabel. She had been checking on him every hour since he fell asleep. "I'm sorry I didn't come straight out," he said. "I was just trying to clear some cobwebs."

"Stay as long as you wish, my Lord," said Annabel. "I'll let Master Geoffrey know that you have woken." She turned toward the hallway.

"Annabel," he said.

She stopped. "Yes, my Lord."

"I'm sorry for coming here this morning in such a state."

She smiled. For the first time since he became Lord of Heshire, she could see beyond the title of Lord and rank of magician. "Don't worry about it. I was young once, you know. The stories I could tell." She chuckled.

"It wasn't proper for me to come here, and for you all to see me like that."

"May I be frank, my Lord?" she asked.

"Please do." It would be nice if someone would be, he thought.

"I've taken care of you since birth, and as far as I can remember, you're still a human. And humans do make mistakes. I don't care if you're a magician, a Lord, a healer, or a farmer. You're going to do things that you regret, especially when you're young."

"And how do I begin to make amends for those things?"

"You've already started." She smiled and walked out of the room. "Oh!" she called from the hallway before returning to the door. "Would you like me to make your bacon now?"

Lord Barton twisted his face and put a hand over his stomach. "Did I ask for bacon?"

"You certainly did, my Lord. You told Master Geoffrey you wanted him to save you some."

"I did, huh?"

"I saved you some too. I could fry it now. It'll only take a few minutes."

"While I love your bacon, I believe I'll take you up on it on another day."

"Well, then perhaps a nice piece of bread would do the trick for now."

"It certainly would."

"I'll bring you a cup of cider as well."

"Thank you, Annabel."

"You're welcome. Master Geoffrey will be in short-ly."

Geoffrey was pulling weeds in his rose garden when Annabel let him know that Lord Barton had awakened. This was the first time he had been able to work in the garden in over a month. Even though Lord Barton had a groundskeeper who took care of everything, he rather enjoyed the work because it was relaxing, and it gave him a much-deserved mental break.

He put his trowel on the ground and brushed himself off. He would prefer to change into more suitable clothes, but Lord Barton needed to talk to him about something important, and he didn't want to keep him waiting.

The first stop, however, was the kitchen. Earlier in the day, he had Aidan pull some Abilica and Hessroot out of the herb garden which had been drying in the oven ever since. He ground the dried herbs to a fine powder in his mortar and pestle, and then stirred the powder in a cup of hot water. He added some cinnamon and sugar for taste and took the cup with him to the library.

Lord Barton sat on the couch holding his head in his hands. The throbbing was worse, and reading didn't make it any better. He was content to sit in silence and was in no hurry to talk to anyone, but there were important things to discuss, and Geoffrey was the only person in Heshire who he could trust.

"My Lord?" Geoffrey asked. He opened the

library's door slowly just in case the young magician had fallen back to sleep.

"Geoffrey, please come in." He didn't bother to stand, thinking that the healer would certainly understand his discomfort at the moment. "I would like to apologize for inconveniencing you this morning. I was…"

"It was no inconvenience, my Lord. You know my home is your home."

"It wasn't right for me to be that way around you and Aidan."

"Aidan? He's a man just as you. Young, but of the age nonetheless."

Lord Barton smiled. "I remember playing with him when I was a child. He's two years younger than me, right?"

"That's right. Now forget about all that nonsense. After all, I pulled you from your mother's womb, and I've seen you in far worse circumstances."

"You mean that time I accidentally turned my skin red?" He laughed. "I was barely an apprentice then… had no idea how to use my power."

Geoffrey handed him the mug. "Drink this. It'll make you feel better in a few minutes." He remembered the young magician's accident. He was supposed to be practicing on an old shirt, but he decided to cast the spell while looking in a mirror. Instead of changing the color of the shirt, he changed the color of his skin. Lord Barton was too afraid to tell his father, so he snuck to Geoffrey's house and hid until the healer returned.

Lord Barton sipped the medicine. It wasn't so hot, so he turned the mug up and drank in big gulps, hoping it would take effect sooner than later. "I need your counsel," he said after he finished the drink. He put the empty mug on the table and leaned back on the couch waiting for his head to calm down.

"What would you like to talk about, my Lord?"

"Please," said Lord Barton. "Let's dispense of the formality. I need the advice of someone I look up to."

Geoffrey had always respected the hierarchy. And even though he was old enough to be Lord Barton's father, he was the ruler of Heshire and all its lands, and required respect, regardless of his age. "Whatever you need, I'll be happy to listen. I just hope I can be helpful." He hoped this conversation would shed some light on everything that happened last night. It all seemed like a bad dream now, but he couldn't get it off his mind. The only thing that calmed him so far was the time he spent with his roses, and he strongly suspected that Lord Barton's binge was his attempt to rid the same problems from his mind.

"I wasn't being honest with you about everything," said Lord Barton.

Geoffrey nodded his head. "I didn't think I was being told everything."

"Those soldiers were the victims of magic...a very powerful magic from a very bad man."

"Black magic?" Geoffrey wasn't going to mince his words. If Lord Barton wanted to dispense with formality, then he was going to get right to the heart of the matter.

"I suspect so. I couldn't do anything to help them, and believe me, I tried. It was greater than anything I've ever seen."

"What about the man the guards brought in?"

"Lord Nilet, the Emperor's deputy."

"Has his condition improved?" Geoffrey didn't know what was wrong with the man, but he assumed he was not doing well.

"No. He's unresponsive and has been since Druck struck him with some spell." He hoped he was doing the right thing by telling Geoffrey all of this. He knew the Emperor would not want the Healer to know state's affairs, but since Lord Griswold left for Tarsus, things have come up, and he needed someone to talk to.

"Druck?"

"He took control of Sarcus after his father died earlier this year. I know very little about him other than the fact that he's been settling an old grudge with Parthage."

Geoffrey nodded. "That war's been going on for years."

"Yes, but his father had negotiated a peace. The war began over a minor dispute, and it was resolved. Now that Druck has taken power, he's launched an assault. The Emperor sent Lord Nilet to Sarcus to meet with Druck. I don't know anything more than that."

"Is there anything else you want to share with me?"

Lord Barton stood and went to the bookshelf. He glanced over the collection and pulled out a dusty book and then opened it to the first page. "Here, see for yourself." He handed the book to Geoffrey.

Geoffrey turned the book over. It was one of his father's journals and had sat on the bookshelf since his death, untouched until now. "Healing against black magic," said Geoffrey. He flipped through the pages, reading bits and pieces as he went. His father had re-corded many spells that he'd seen during the war with Sarcus and had created remedies for each spell. "I've never seen this before. How did you…"

"I was nosy in my youth. I found it lying behind a stack of books on your shelf one day, and I took it home and read it." He turned around and stared at the fireplace. "I was intrigued by black magic, or at least the stories I'd heard about the council of magi-cians. When my father found the book, he punished me and told me to return it immediately. I was afraid to tell you, so I snuck back in one day and put it back. Imagine my surprise to see it still sitting where I left it."

"Are you certain that Druck has turned?"

"Those spells were powerful. I couldn't help those poor men, and everything I've tried on Lord Nilet has failed." He rubbed the back of his neck. "Every-thing."

"What about the Emperor? Do you think he can reverse the spell?"

"Griswold is heading to Tarsus as we speak, but I have my doubts. My forefathers were known for their ability to counter magic. The power lies in my cloak, but it's ineffectual, as is everything I've been taught. Why do you think my grandfather was given this land? It's so close to the border, and Leopold wanted a magician here who could thwart any magic leveled against Gornia."

Geoffrey didn't know any of this about Lord Barton or his family. "So, your powers are no good against his magic?"

"The magic we know, yes. But black magic grows,

and Druck has new powers."

"His father would certainly have not allowed it."

"Rumor has it that he had a falling out with his father many years ago and moved to a country estate in the east. He could have practiced without ever being caught."

Geoffrey closed the book and held it tightly in his hand. He would begin reading it soon, he thought. He figured that his father had never given him the manual because black magic was thought to be a thing of the past. He would have to learn the spells and the remedies as soon as possible, and he needed to find out how his father came up with them so he could use the same process against new spells. "Can I do anything to help?"

"Read that book and see if you find anything that could help Lord Nilet. It will be at least three weeks before I hear anything from Griswold, and I fear we don't have that much time."

"I'll start today."

"Right now, if you could. If Druck is up to something, he won't wait to strike, so time's of the essence." Lord Barton reached over and patted Geoffrey's arm. "You have always been like a father to me, and that's why I'm confiding in you. I trust you will share this information with no one."

"Aidan needs to know. He needs to know how to deal with black magic as well, especially if something happens to me."

Lord Barton rubbed his chin. "Will he be able to keep quiet?"

"Certainly. Healers know many things about every person under their care, and they're forbidden to reveal anything. He's trustworthy."

"Then fill him in." He walked towards the door. "Oh, speaking of Aidan, my sister is coming for a few days. I know she'd love to see him…and you. Would you two care to join us for dinner?"

"We would love to."

"I know it's dreadful timing, but she left before any of this happened, and I couldn't turn her away."

"Not at all. Her company will be a delightful detour from everything."

"I've got to figure out how I'm going to explain this mess to her. She's so hot-headed that she might just give Druck a piece of her mind right from the start."

Geoffrey laughed. "Red heads."

Lord Barton laughed chuckled. "Please come through the front door from now on. I don't want anyone thinking my healer is a servant, especially Annabel. She'll never let me hear the end of it."

"We will." As soon as he left, Geoffrey opened the book. He'd read until Aidan got back from the amputation, and then he'd try to explain it all to him.

Sweat rolled off Aidan's forehead. He'd been fighting the old man for hours, it seemed, and now was not the time for the farmer to resist. "You have to hold still!" he demanded. The house, if he could call it that, was as hot as a grain oven, and his fingers were so slippery that holding the knife steady was impossible, especially while having to pin the man's arm still.

"You're hurting me!" screamed the old man.

"Where's your father?!" Blood poured from the wound. He'd cut it halfway off when he was sharpening the blades on his plow, and he had tried to heal it himself by pouring corn liquor on it and wrapping it with dirty old linens he'd cut into strips. After five days of that, his finger turned green, and he was forced to have his neighbor go get help.

Aidan put his bloody fingers under the man's chin and pushed up so the man would look him in the eyes. "I'm perfectly capable of helping you, but you've got to hold still. I can't sew it shut if I don't have good skin to work with, so I've got to take more of the finger off."

"It's hurting! I thought you said that powder would take the pain away!"

Aidan went back to work on the finger. "It is! You wouldn't be awake right now if it wasn't working!" He didn't know how his father had done it by himself for so many years. He'd always known that he'd be alone once he became a healer, but he had no idea that it would be this difficult. Perhaps his father should have come on this one, he thought. He'd done many amputations over the past few years, but he always had his father with him as a guide and assistant. Doing it by himself was a different experience altogether.

"Can't you give me more of that stuff?!" the old man cried. "It hurts too bad!"

Aidan wiped the sweat off his head, leaving a trail of blood above his eyebrows. "No! I can't. You wouldn't be hurting so much if you'd have come to us before now. The infection made it worse!"

"I didn't go to you because I knew it would hurt like hell!" screamed the farmer. "Now give me more

77

of your magic!"

"Magic won't help you! The 'magic' you're yelling about will kill you if you take any more!" He wasn't about to tell the old man that he didn't know the magic, or he would certainly get up and run out the door like he'd done twice already. "Now hold still! You're acting like a baby!"

All of a sudden, the farmer sat quietly. Aidan glanced up and noticed that the man looked afraid, but he could tell that it had nothing to do with the rotting finger. He pulled the knife away from the bone. "What's wrong?"

"You...your..." The man lifted his other hand and pointed feebly at Aidan. "Your eyes...they turned as black as coal."

Aidan shook his head. "It's the powder. Don't worry about it."

The old man shook his finger again. "I know what I saw. Your eyes were solid black...no white at all. Your face glowed too."

Aidan chuckled. "And you said that 'magic' didn't work for you. I guess you're wrong." He put the knife back on the bone and began to saw once again, this time without any resistance.

When he finally removed the short tip of healthy bone, he was able to pull the flap of skin over the stump and sew it shut. He covered it with an herbal balm, rubbing it onto the stitching. He finished by wrapping the old man's hand with a clean bandage. "Here, these are for you." He handed the man a stack of bandages and a small jar of balm. "Change the bandage once a day for a week. When you do, rub this balm over the stitches. You'll be fine after that."

"A healer magician," said the old man.

"What did you say?" asked Aidan.

"You're a magician. I've seen it before."

"What have you seen before?"

"The eyes...the glow on your face...you have magical powers."

Aidan chuckled. "It'll wear off by tonight. Don't go back to the fields until your head is cleared up, you hear?"

The old man stood. "Listen to me! I know what I'm talking about. I've been around for a long time, and I've seen my fair share of magicians."

"I'm an apprentice. I don't have any magical powers."

"Oh yes you do! You'll find out one day. Just remember I told you first." He stumbled back to a bed in the corner of the room and sat down. "Shut the door when you leave, sorcerer." He started to laugh.

Aidan closed the door. He'd have to be careful about how much Parthworm he put in the next batch of pain reliever. "I have to tell dad about this one," he mumbled while getting on his horse.

Chapter 10

Geoffrey spent the entire afternoon reading his father's journal. He read through every spell, and he studied each remedy. He hoped he would find something that would help him heal Lord Nilet, but he knew the chances of that were slim. Healers just couldn't help magicians who had been affected by magic. It wasn't possible. The book was filled with outstanding information, things that he wished his father had shared with him when he was younger. Although he had to admit that he'd never seen the effects of black magic until now, he wished he would have known all of this just in case.

Leafing from page to page, he couldn't find anything that resembled what those soldiers had. He would have felt horrible if the cure was in this book. But there were many other spells that did nasty things to people. One spell he found turned people into stone slowly and painfully. Another caused a person's skin to melt right off his body. There was even one that turned a person into a farm animal. These were stories the poets praised, but he just assumed they were all made up. Now, he was becoming very familiar with a reality that people had to face over a hundred years ago.

The one that intrigued him the most was a viral incantation that spread disease among a large group of people. His father described it as a weakening spell, intended to target a region before an attack to make it more vulnerable. Once the spell was cast, people would succumb to a host of diseases resulting in a high, uncontrollable fever. He had seen an increase in feverish illnesses over the past six months, and he wondered if Druck had anything to do with it.

Aidan ran down the hallway to tell his father about the amputation. He was excited that he'd performed his first major procedure by himself, and he was sure that his father would be proud of him.

Geoffrey heard the front door slam and the heavy footsteps across the stone floor, and he had already turned around when Aidan bounded through the door. "Well, how did it go?"

Aidan had to catch his breath before talking. "It was fantastic!" he said excitedly.

Geoffrey laughed. "I've never thought about an amputation as being 'fantastic.' It went well then?"

Aidan grinned. "It sure did. I mean, the old man was a bear to work on. He kept pulling his hand away and yelling at me, but I finally convinced him to calm down, and I was able to finish with no problem!"

Geoffrey didn't respond. He just stared at Aidan's face.

"What's the matter?" asked Aidan. He thought about what the farmer told him and wondered if his father was seeing something unusual too.

"You've got blood on your forehead." He laughed.

Aidan went to the mirror and looked at his face. His eyebrows were caked in dry blood, and his forehead had red finger streaks all over it. "Is that why the guards were laughing at me in the stable?"

"I suppose so," replied his father. "Rule number eight...always wash off before leaving." He laughed again. He remembered when he'd done the same thing when he was young, and his wife almost passed out when he came home. "I needed that." He started laughing again. "Thank you!"

Aidan didn't see the humor in it. He was embarrassed by the slip up. The old man had been talking so much gibberish that he had completely forgotten to clean up before leaving. "I'd better get this off," he said.

Geoffrey finally calmed down. "Hold on. Don't leave yet. Lord Barton's invited us to dinner tonight. Amelia's back, and he thought you two would like to get together. I suppose you'll want a bath before then."

Aidan stared blankly into the mirror. It had been almost a year since he'd seen her. She left to live with her uncle in Plackith so she could finish her education. She was only partially through with her apprenticeship when her father died, and Lord Barton wasn't experienced enough to finish it with her, so she had to leave.

The two of them had always been close because they were the same age. Lord Barton was a little older, and although he did play with him some, he never had the bond that he shared with Amelia. He was certain he loved her when she left, and the only thing that kept her off his mind during her absence was his work. Now, all of those feelings welled up inside him once again.

"Aidan?" asked his father. "Aidan?"

"Yes, I do want to take a bath," he replied softly.

Geoffrey suspected the two of them were in love, so he understood why his son had faded out so quickly. "We don't have to be there until later. I need to talk to you about something first."

Aidan pulled himself away from the mirror and sat on the couch. "I did everything else right," he said. "He'll be fine."

"I know you did. I don't want to talk to you about the finger."

Aidan was relieved. "Oh, alright." He relaxed and leaned back on the couch, pulling a pillow across his lap and holding it tightly. "What do you want to talk about?"

"Lord Barton shared some information with me earlier this afternoon that we thought you needed to know."

"How is he doing?"

"He was suffering a little, but he was fine."

Aidan laughed. "Did he get his bacon?"

"No," Geoffrey chuckled. "He didn't want any after all." Geoffrey leaned forward. "It's important, Aidan. I need you to listen."

Aidan threw the pillow down and bent forward. "I'm listening." As serious as his father had become, he had a feeling that it had something to do with the conversation they'd had the night before.

"It was black magic."

"The soldiers?"

"Yes. Lord Barton fears that Druck did it. Apparently, he's been practicing black magic for years, and no one knew. He's become very powerful for his age, and Lord Barton fears that he wants to invade Gornia."

"Why would he break the treaty? It's been so many years."

"He doesn't know, but the two soldiers and Lord Nilet…"

"Lord Nilet? You mean THE Lord Nilet?"

"Yes. They were on a mission to meet with Druck. Lord Barton doesn't know anything about this meeting but he thinks it must have gone poorly."

"I know what happened to the soldiers, but what about Lord Nilet?"

"He's apparently alive but in some sort of coma."

"Can Lord Barton do anything to help him?"

"Nothing has worked. He couldn't even help the two soldiers."

"He tried?"

"He said so."

Aidan couldn't believe what he was hearing. The treaty hadn't ever been broken. The two countries had lived in peace for over one hundred years. Why would Druck want to start another war? Had he gone mad with black magic? "What can be done?"

"Lord Griswold left for Tarsus last night to speak to the Emperor. He won't return for several weeks, so we've got to try anything we can to heal Lord Nilet. Lord Barton fears that we're on the brink of war."

"How can we help? Healing a magician affected by magic is not possible. If he can't do it, maybe another magician can."

"That brings me to my greatest fear. Lord Barton is the one they'd turn to for help, and he can't do anything."

"Why him?"

"His power contains a thousand years worth of remedies against magical spells."

"You're saying he's a healer for magicians?"

"As I understand it."

Aidan threw himself on the couch. "That's not

good."

Annabel laid out their finest clothes before heading to the manor herself. Lord Barton asked if she would do the honor of preparing the special meal that evening, and she gladly accepted. She had been the main cook for the Lord's family for many years until she moved in with Geoffrey and Aidan. She looked forward to seeing Amelia as much as anyone because she practically raised her from birth after her mother passed away.

Aidan slowly dressed in front of the mirror because he didn't want to wrinkle his pants or shirt. He was glad Annabel put out his green trousers and jacket. They were his favorite clothes, and he had always been told that green looked good on him. After dressing, he focused on his hair. Unlike most boys his age, he preferred to keep his hair short. Long hair just got in his way, especially when he was amputating a limb or doing some other bloody task, so he had it cut. He knew it looked odd for a young man, but that didn't matter to him. He was a healer, and he had to think about that first.

After brushing every hair in place, he leaned forward and stared closely at his eyes. He'd forgotten to tell his father what the old man said, but since it was such nonsense, he figured that he would just keep it to himself. After all, there were more important things to think discuss. He didn't see anything unusual about his eyes. They were as brown as ever, a fitting match to his hair. The old man was just hallucinating.

"Took you long enough," said Geoffrey. "I've been waiting for ten minutes. I was getting ready to pull you out." He punched Aidan softly on the shoulder. "You look fine."

"I just took a long bath," Aidan stated. "Blood doesn't clean off so easily."

Geoffrey shook his head and opened the door. "Let's go before they eat without us."

Lord Barton's dining room was much larger than the one in Geoffrey's house. It had a long mahogany table that sat twelve people comfortably. A large chandelier with over fifty candles hung above the table on an iron chain. The room's one entrance was flanked by two serving tables and a china cabinet that was full of old plates and crystal wine glasses.

By the time they arrived, the table had been set for the four of them. Since Amelia left, he rarely used this room, preferring to take his meals in the library instead. He only ate here when he had a special guest or when his sister came to visit, and lately, those were rare occasions.

Karl led the two men to the sitting room. Amelia was sitting in a chair with her back to the door, and Lord Barton was standing by the window looking south toward Sarcus. Aidan stood briefly in the doorway and stared at her hair. She had the prettiest red hair. It was longer than he remembered, but it was as perfectly combed as it was the day she left.

"Go to her," said Geoffrey quietly. He sensed that Aidan was a little nervous.

Aidan walked up behind her and cleared his throat. As soon as she saw him, her eyes lit up with delight, and she jumped out of the chair and hugged him.

"I've missed you so much," she said, and she kissed him on the neck. He returned the favor, and they hugged harder. This feels right, he thought. He didn't want to let go.

"I've missed you too," he said. "I wish you could come back more often." She pulled away from him and grabbed his hands to get a better look at him. "You look the same as you did when I left. I can see that Annabel's taking care of you."

He gazed into her emerald eyes. They were so beautiful that they could put any man in a trance. And her skin…her alabaster skin…she was definitely the most beautiful woman he'd ever seen. She was the perfect beauty and the perfect person, and that made her the right person for him. There was no doubt – he was in love.

Lord Barton walked beside them and stuck out his hand to Aidan. "I hate to break up you two love birds, but it's good to see you tonight."

Amelia slapped her brother's shoulder. "You're too much!"

"Thank you for inviting us."

"You're welcome. Would you care for some brandy?"

Aidan stared into Amelia's eyes. He couldn't take them off of her. She seemed content to stare back as well. "I'll have what you're having, my Lord."

Lord Barton turned to Karl. "He'll have water."

Aidan couldn't help but snicker. Perhaps he'd had

his fill of brandy for a while, he thought.

"How has the year been for you?" she asked.

"It's been very busy. I've been doing well, though. My father's been a good teacher." He looked over at him and nodded. "How has it been with your uncle?"

She smiled half-heartedly. "I miss being here. I wish I could finish with my brother, but my uncle says he's not ready for a high apprentice, so I must go back."

"How much longer do you have?"

"At least two more years. And you?"

"About the same or maybe a little less. I don't know. It depends upon my father. Is your uncle treating you well?"

"He's difficult but fair. I'm supposed to be able to throw fire right now, but the most I can manage is a little spark. I know he's frustrated with me, so he sent me here for a little break. He thinks it'll do me good." She smiled. "I think he's the one who needs the break."

"Maybe Lord Barton can help you."

"I might ask him."

She squeezed his hand tightly pulled him to the window behind the desk. Pulling back the drapes, she pointed at the stable on the right side of the courtyard. "Do you remember when…?"

Aidan smiled and leaned into her ear. "I could never forget."

"What are you two talking about?" His father stood behind them, holding a glass of water for his son. He had a big grin on his face.

"Nothing," said Amelia. She winked Aidan and turned towards the window.

"Nothing," said Aidan. "Just remembering old times, that's all." He grabbed the glass and took a sip of water.

"You must be talking about the time when you two decided that jumping out of the loft onto bales of hay was a good idea."

"Oh yes, that's what we were talking about," replied Amelia. She squeezed Aidan's hand tightly.

"Got it right," Aidan said.

"Well, as I recall, I had to treat both of you for broken ankles." He knew they weren't talking about that time, but he thought he'd play with them nonetheless.

Amelia and Aidan stared out of the window and talked quietly to one another for half an hour, never letting go of each other's hand. Lord Barton and Geoffrey were engaged in an important conversation at the fireplace anyway, so they decided to give them space while they enjoyed theirs.

The four diners took a seat at the table at eight o'clock sharp. Annabel had prepared a roasted pig, potatoes, corn, and rice pudding, and she even baked a cake for dessert. Lord Barton stood. "This is a fine meal, Annabel. Thank you."

"It was an honor, my Lord."

He put his hands over the table and rolled his wrists. A place setting with plates, utensils, and a glass appeared at the head of the table. "Then it would be my honor if you would join us."

Annabel's eyes lit up. "Thank you, my Lord. I don't know if…"

"I don't want to hear it, Annabel," said Amelia. "You're part of our family. Anyway, we know you're used to eating with Geoffrey and Aidan. We wouldn't have it any other way."

"Thank you. Thank you everyone. You are the best family in the world."

"Now, if Amelia would please stand," said Lord Barton.

She looked puzzled. She knew he was up to something, and she couldn't wait to see what he was planning. "You're not going to change me into a chicken again, are you?"

Everyone broke out in laughter. He had accidentally done that when he had just become an apprentice, or at least that's what he told everyone. Amelia knew he'd done it on purpose, though, but she never told anyone, especially her father.

He winked at her. "You know that was an accident. Anyway, father had you out of the chicken house in no time!"

Aidan almost fell out of his chair. He remembered her father frantically looking for the chicken with the necklace wrapped around its neck. It was the funniest thing he had ever seen.

"No. I want you to show off a little for us. It's getting dark in here, and we need a little light."

Amelia frantically shook her head. "You really don't want me doing that. Why don't you do it?"

"Nonsense. You're ready for it."

She leaned over the table. "I was meaning to talk to you about that. I really need a little practice."

"Try. It won't hurt anything. They're simple candles."

Aidan knew why she was scared. "Perhaps she's a little tired."

"Yes, that's it. I'm exhausted. I think I should wait until another day."

Lord Barton shook his head. "It's not that difficult, Amelia. I'm proud of you, and I want everyone to see what you've been learning."

Amelia knew that she shouldn't try, but she didn't want to disappoint or embarrass her brother either. She closed her eyes and put her hand on Aidan's shoulder. "Alright," she reluctantly agreed. "I'll light them."

Aidan wasn't sure that she should be doing this if she'd been having problems at her uncle's. He knew the pressure she was feeling, and he wanted to stand up and say enough. But it was her decision, and he respected that.

She pointed her finger at the candelabra and summoned the spell in her head. Nothing happened for a few seconds, but then a small ball of fire left the tip of her finger and spiraled in the air towards the closest candle. It looked innocuous at first, but when it hit the candle, it exploded into a great ball of fire that engulfed the entire ceiling of the room. Everyone at the table jumped under the table for cover.

Lord Barton looked at his sister in surprise. "I guess I should have listened to you," he said.

She nodded. "I was going to tell you that I need your help with that."

He pointed his finger, twirled it around in tiny circles, and raised it towards the top of the table. A cold wind blew hard through the room and put the fire out in a few seconds. "I guess we'll be eating on the patio tonight," he said, and he walked out of the dining room in a daze.

After dinner, the four retired to the library to discuss the situation regarding Lord Nilet and Druck. Lord Barton had already told Amelia what he told Geoffrey, but he had some new information that he wanted to share with everyone. He'd spent the afternoon combing through his father's journals, and he thought he found a possible answer to the problem, although he knew it was a long-shot.

Lord Barton's father had been a quasi-historian. Growing up under the tutelage of the man who was front and center in most battles of the great war, he had reason to be interested in all of the stories he'd heard. Instead of idly listening to his father, he took time to record them in great detail. Neither Lord Barton nor Amelia showed much interest in their grandfather's stories, and the journals collected dust on the bookshelves over the years. He thought it was quite interesting that he had found a jewel in his own library as he had found a jewel in Geoffrey's library so many years before. Such was fate. Perhaps these finds were meant to be at this important junction in Gornia's history, he thought.

Lord Barton poured everyone a glass of wine from his cellar, and he raised his glass to toast. "To friends and family," he said.

"To friends and family," everyone repeated as they touched glasses.

After they took a few sips of wine, he stood. "We

need to talk." He looked at Aidan and Amelia. "You two will have your time, I promise. You all know by now what we're up against. Griswold should be half-way to Tarsus by now, but he will not be given a chance to meet with a ranking official for several days. I know the system well enough to know that it will take time. When he is granted an audience with an official, it will take several more days to reach the Emperor. Once the Emperor is informed, he will convene his committee of delegates to discuss the matter, and that may take several weeks." He paused and took a deep breath. "So, what I'm trying to say is that it will be several weeks before we hear back from him." He paused again. "That may be too long."

"And you're sure you can't counter the spell?" asked Amelia.

"Amelia, I've told you at least three times...I've done everything I can do. Nothing works."

"Then what are our options?" asked Geoffrey. "I read through my father's notes on black magic, and there's nothing in there that will help us."

"What notes?" asked Aidan.

"I didn't have a chance to tell you. They're some notes he took during the war – cures for some black magic spells."

Lord Barton pulled a stack of journals from a shelf at the back of the room, and he laid them on the table beside Aidan. "I have something that might be of interest." He handed the top book to Geoffrey. "You probably know of my father's interest in history and how he meticulously recorded everything my grandfather told him. There's a lot of uninteresting facts in most of the journals, but this one, in particular, has some hopeful relevance to us."

Amelia leaned over as Geoffrey flipped through the pages. There were hundreds of pages of handwritten notes in each journal.

"Father recorded one story at the back of the book." He took the book from Geoffrey's hands and turned to one of the last pages. "Here it is." He handed it back to Geoffrey. "Would you read it aloud?"

"Sure," he said.

The Healer Magician

A minor Sarcugian magician who went by the name Gorn or Garn, I cannot remember, was captured at the Battle of Slint. I questioned him for several hours about the whereabouts of the council of magicians, but he did not know where they were. Such was our fortune at the time. He was a young magician and rather weak, and I was able to read his mind quite easily. He knew nothing important, so I was about to send him to the prison camp in Tarsus when I came across an interesting tidbit hidden at the edge of his consciousness. I suppose he was trying to hide it from me, and that's why I thought it important to note. In the end, though, it helped us little.

He had apparently been given the task of finding a magician named...

oh, I cannot remember his name. It was so long ago, and my notes were destroyed after the treaty was signed. Anyway, this particular magician must have been powerful because the council wanted to find him quickly. He was a Sarcugian, but he was opposed to the war. He especially despised black magic, if I correctly recall. He refused to support the council, and he was accused of conspiring against Sarcus by healing all of those who were afflicted by their spells. I distinctly remember seeing that he was both a Healer and a Magician, which was something unheard of at that time, just as it's unheard of now. No one has ever had the power of both since the beginning of time, but the council was convinced that he did, so they pursued him.

He fled the council and was thought to be hiding in the Crokus Mountains in northern Sarcus disguised as a hermit. They received reports that he married a local woman and had a son, but they could never find him.

Son, if this information was true, and I have no doubt the Sarcugians believed it so, then they were chasing the most powerful man who ever lived… an anomaly of everything we thought possible. He would have been able to cure disease, reverse magical spells, and cure the black magic plague that swept through both lands during the war. Our family has always had the ability to counter magic, but our powers are restricted to white magic, and they work only on magicians. If he lived, he would have been the cure for everything. It is too bad that he chose to go into hiding instead of joining us. The war would have ended much sooner had he had. Now, I would like to tell you about my friend, Protus…

Geoffrey closed the book. Everyone stood in silence for several seconds as they thought about its relevance to their situation.

"Do you see why I'm so excited?" Lord Barton asked. "I found this early in the afternoon, and I've been dying to tell you about it all day."

"A healer magician," said Aidan. "If it's true, then he'd be unlike anyone who was ever born. The power he'd have."

Geoffrey handed the book back to Lord Barton and took a large gulp of wine. "The story mentioned that he had a son. His son would have been granted the same powers, and his son's son, and so on. We have to assume that he would train his children and his children's children in the ways of the magician and healer."

Amelia took the book from her brother and flipped to the entry at the back of the journal. "You mean the answer to Lord Nilet's problem lies on the other side of the Elbe?"

"It's more than that," said Lord Barton. "If he was who grandfather said he was, and if Geoffrey's theory is true, then his bloodline is the only one that could deal Druck a decisive defeat. If we could find his grandchild and convince him to join us, then we could destroy Druck before he has a chance to attack."

"And how do you suppose we find him?" asked Amelia. "The Crokus mountain range runs for at least three hundred legions. You read the account...even the Sarcugians couldn't find him. What makes you think we could...one hundred years later?!"

The room was silent for a few seconds. She was right. How would they find one person in all those mountains with nothing more than an old account from an old man's collection of stories?

Geoffrey nodded his head as if he had it figured out. "Lord Barton, you made a good point when you talked about the timing of finding some forgotten journals in my library and yours. Perhaps it's coincidence, but when you reach my age, you learn that everything has a purpose whether you want to believe it or not. We're definitely facing a crisis, and it's unfolding before our very eyes. And now we have a possible solution that's been handed down to us from our fathers. I don't know about you three, but I believe that we have to follow our instincts in this matter."

Lord Barton put his hand on Geoffrey's shoulder to thank him for speaking. "My instinct tells me that we have to look for him. If we don't, then we'll spend the rest of our lives wondering if we did everything we could to save Gornia."

"I agree," said Geoffrey. "I say we look. If fate has served us so far, then it will continue to serve us if we follow its path."

Aidan and Amelia held each other's hand tightly. Aidan didn't want to contradict his father, and Amelia didn't want to insult her brother. But neither were convinced.

"I just don't know about all of this. It flies in the face of everything I've been taught about magic and healing," said Aidan.

"It does seem far-fetched," agreed Amelia.

Lord Barton turned to the two. "I don't hold anything against either of you for your doubts. Believe me, there's a part of me that believes this is a myth, but the greater part of me thinks there's a good chance that grandfather was right. Why would he lie?"

"He wouldn't lie, but there are too many issues with the story," said Amelia. "To begin with, he was already an old man when he told father, and the war had been over for many years. Also, you have to admit that he got the information from a Sarcugian who could have been setting a trap. And if it wasn't that all you have is a Sarcugian myth! They never found him, right? How do we know he really existed?"

Aidan agreed. "I think the chances are slim that he existed at all. It's even more unlikely that we'll find any offspring if he did. We'd be risking our necks for nothing."

"Do you think that saving the lives of thousands of Gornians would be for nothing? We have an opportunity here, and we have to act upon it," said Geoffrey.

"Believe what you may, but if we all don't go, then none of us go," said Lord Barton. I can't ask my guards. They are too thinned out already. I need them here to protect the village if anything happens. We must be the ones to go."

"You don't have to give us an answer right now," Geoffrey said. "But I believe we need to know your decision by the morning. I'm convinced this is the right thing to do. I know Lord Barton is as well."

"We'll let you know after breakfast," said Amelia. She tightened her grip around Aidan's hand and headed for the door. "I need some fresh air. Let's take a walk."

Lord Barton and Geoffrey remained in the library to plan the journey. They were confident the two would make the right decision. If fate had led them this far, then fate would lead those two to follow. It wasn't difficult to believe in fate either. Since Druck had dived so deeply into black magic, he had stirred the order of the universe, and it had a way of correcting itself eventually.

Chapter 11

It was a good night for a walk. The stars were out, the moon was full and bright, and the cool north breeze was a refreshing departure from southern Gornia's typically hot and humid climate.

It rarely rained because the Crokus Mountains seemed to deflect storm fronts around the sleepy village, and farmers had to rely upon irrigation canals dug to the river to water their crops.

As a result, some of the prettiest parts of the countryside were around the irrigation canals. Tall oaks and pines thrived near the wide canals that led to the larger farms, and peasant women were apt to plant Biscus, Fornt, and Portical plants along the banks. The brightly colored flowers glowed yellow and white in the moonlight, and their sweet fragrance perfumed the air. Best of all, the water's gentle flow over the river boulders created a relaxing melody in the quiet of the night.

Amelia and Aidan sat against a thick oak and watched the moon's reflection over the bubbling waters of the village canal. It was the largest canal in all of Heshire, and it was close enough to the manor to provide an occasional secluded escape.

Village guards usually herded lovers back inside the walls after dark because Lord Barton feared the Sarcugians would slip over the river to kidnap helpless people, but it had never happened, and Amelia thought the paranoia was an extreme carry-over of her father's fears. She had come here by herself for many years, and nothing ever happened to her. It didn't take her long to find an easy way around the guards either. A few minutes of proper timing, and a convenient trap door in the wall at the back of the courtyard were all they needed to get out of the village.

Aidan had come here with her a couple of times in the past, but none of them were for romantic encounters. Even though they felt strongly for one another, they had never shared an intimate moment or even a long, deep kiss. It wasn't because they didn't want to, but by the time they figured out that their feelings for one another, she moved to her uncle's estate.

"Remember when we came out here last summer?" asked Amelia. "It was a night very much like tonight." She reached down to pick a small Portical flower she saw on the ground. She sniffed it before throwing it in the water to watch it float downstream in the moonlight.

"It sure was," said Aidan. He wanted to tell her how he almost reached over to kiss her that night, but he wasn't sure how she'd respond. He wasn't confident she felt the same way for him as he did for her, so he waited for the right time. Although they'd held hands for what seemed like the entire night, he couldn't decide if that was a sign of romantic affection or a close friendship.

They watched the flower float down the canal until it disappeared around a bend, then they both leaned back against the trunk of the oak. Amelia left her coat at the manor, and Aidan could feel the goose bumps on her arm. "You're cold," he said. He put his arm around her shoulders and pulled her close to him. Perhaps this would be the right time to kiss her, he thought.

"How about you?" she asked.

"It is a little cool out here."

"Do you want me to make a fire?"

"Not if you don't want to burn the village down," said Aidan as he laughed. He was getting very comfortable with this situation. He felt like things were going to move forward very soon, and he was filled with anticipation.

Amelia started rubbing her finger over his right arm, tracing pretend circles and lines from his elbow to the top of his hand. "There is something that I can do," she said.

Aidan's heart started pounding in his chest. Was this it? He turned his head and looked into her eyes. "What?"

She pulled out of his embrace and turned to face him. "This." She pointed her finger, closed her eyes, and mumbled something he couldn't understand. The tip of her finger started to glow orange, and after a few seconds, it was as bright as a candle's flame. She opened her eyes, touched his arm and started drawing the same circles and lines she had before. At first, he didn't feel anything unusual, but then it hit him. Every nerve in his arm came alive with the sensation of being tickled in his most sensitive spots. He started laughing so hard that he fell backwards. He had never felt so ticklish in his life, especially on his arm.

As he tried to roll away, Amelia hopped on top of him and straddled his hips with her legs. She wasn't going to let him get away that easily.

"Stop it!" he cried between short breaths. "I can't breathe!"

After she thought he'd had enough, she pulled her

finger off of his arm. It stopped glowing immediately. She bent over and looked into his eyes. "Just a little trick I learned from my cousin," she said.

Aidan caught his breath and shook his head. "You're too much! I don't know what you did, but it felt like you were tickling my feet."

She pushed her hips back across his groin and leaned down just a few inches from his face. "That was for the time you pushed me in the river."

"I remember that. We were what? Twelve?"

"Yea, and I was wearing my new riding boots. They got all wet." She puckered her lips as if she were pouting.

"I'm sorry," said Aidan. "We're even now, right?"

Amelia inched her face closer, her lips almost touching his. Her heart was beating hard as she waited to release years of pent up passion and love for the man she wanted. "We're even," she said softly.

As she was about to touch her lips to his, a strange blue light shot across the sky above them, and a strong gust of wind blew through the trees, shredding hundreds of leaves off their branches.

"What was that?!" said Amelia. She pushed to her feet and looked at the sky.

Aidan slammed his fists into the ground out of frustration and then got up and stood beside her. What lousy timing, he thought. "I don't know. It looked like heat lighting, but I didn't really get a good look."

Amelia stared at the sky She moved out of the tree line and stared south. "I didn't specifically see it either, but I know it came from over there." She pointed towards the river.

"Maybe a storm's coming in," Aidan said. "This time of year, they can pop up anytime."

Amelia shook her head. "It's no storm." She pointed at the northern sky. "See, the stars are out."

Aidan looked up. "Then what was it?"

"I don't know."

They scanned the sky on the open road. A deep rumble like the constant sound of thunder shook the ground, and another flash of blue light zigzagged across the sky once again. This time they saw everything. The light came from the Crokus mountains and was bright enough to highlight the ridgeline of the closes mountains in eerie shadows.

"Wow!" shouted Aidan. His heart raced again, but this time out of fear.

"Magic," said Amelia. "It has to be."

Aidan turned to her. "Do you think Druck has something to do with it?"

She shook her head. "I don't know. Something's going on over there, and I don't think it's good."

"Could it be a local magician trying to make rain or something like that?" asked Aidan.

"No. That was no rain spell."

"What did it look like to you?"

"Nothing I've ever seen." She pulled his hand and turned him towards the village. "Come on, we need to tell my brother about it." She pulled him in tow, and she walked quickly towards the wall.

Lord Barton and Geoffrey stared out of the two library windows and looked at the sky. A quick glance across the village proved that everyone had heard the strange noise and saw the odd light streak over them, and there was a great rustling of people in the streets.

"What do you make of it?" asked Geoffrey.

"I don't know," he said. "It was..."

A loud knock at the door startled the two. They swung around, and before the magician could say "enter," the door swung open. It was Annabel. She was in her nightgown and cap and had tears running down her face. "My Lord, Master Geoffrey," she said. "I am so sorry to interrupt you this late, but I'm scared."

Geoffrey ran to her side, put an arm around her, and brought her into the room where he sat her on the couch. Lord Barton handed her his handkerchief and sat beside her. "It's nothing to be concerned about," he said. "It was just a little noise and a light show."

"Yes, my Lord, I heard the thunder and saw the flash of light, but that's not what frightened me."

Geoffrey looked at Lord Barton, and he sat down on her other side. "What happened?"

"I heard footsteps," she said. "It was right after the first sound of thunder. At first, they were soft, and I thought I was hearing things, so I rolled over and tried to go back to sleep. But they kept getting louder..."

Geoffrey gave her a hug. "You're alright Annabel. You're safe now," he said.

"I could tell that someone was coming up the steps. I thought it was you or Aidan at first, but the more I listened, the more I knew it wasn't either of you. I know what you two sound like, and it wasn't you," she repeated.

"Who was it?" asked Lord Barton.

"I finally got the nerve to come out of my room, and I looked down the steps. I didn't see anyone, so I walked down to get a better look." She started to cry.

"Calm down, calm down," reassured Geoffrey. "Did you see anyone?"

"I...I don't know what I saw," she said. "When I got to the bottom of the steps, I looked towards your bedroom doors, and I saw someone standing in front of Aidan's door. He must have heard me because he turned to face me." She leaned forward and put her face in her hands. "All I remember was his eyes."

"What did his eyes look like?" asked Lord Barton.

"They were black," cried Annabel. "I only saw them for a second before he disappeared."

"Did anything unusual happen when he left?" Lord Barton asked.

She looked up and thought. "Yes. That's when I heard the second clap of thunder, and I think I saw another flash of light through the window."

Lord Barton stood and threw open the window. He stuck his head outside and took a deep breath. It's starting, he thought. He didn't know why the magician had gone into Geoffrey's house, but he knew that it had something to do with Druck and Lord Nilet.

Chapter 12

Aidan and Amelia hurried through the courtyard. When they ran past the stables, a guard spotted them and gave chase. The two didn't notice him until he grabbed Aidan by the collar and threw him to the ground.

"Why are you sneaking around the Lord's manor at this time of night?" the guard demanded.

Aidan jerked his shoulders trying to loosen the guard's grip. "Let me go!" he yelled. "I live here."

By the time he spoke, Amelia pushed the guard in the back. "What do you think you're doing?! Get off of him!"

The burly guard looked at Amelia. "My Lady...I...I...I apologize. I was just..." He hadn't moved yet, nor had he removed his hands from Aidan's collar when he answered.

"Remove your hands from him immediately!" she demanded.

The guard slowly stood and reached a hand down to Aidan, helping him get off the ground. For the first time, he saw that he had tackled Aidan. "I am so sorry Master Aidan," he said. He started to brush the dirt and grass off the young healer.

Amelia touched Aidan's cheek. "Are you alright?"

He was shaken but not hurt. "Yea, I'm fine."

Amelia turned to the guard. "What were you thinking?"

"My Lady, we heard a scream come from Master Aidan's house, and then the noise and light in the sky...I thought you were robbers."

"What scream?!" shouted Aidan. He looked across the courtyard at the dark silhouette of his house.

"Miss Annabel. When we came out, she was running to the manor, yelling something about an intruder. We were about to go through the house when you two came running by."

Aidan took a step towards the house, but the guard grabbed his sleeve. "Let us search it before you go in," he said. "It's for your safety."

Amelia put her hand on Aidan's chest. "Your father's still with my brother, and Annabel's probably with them right now. Let's talk to them before you do anything."

"Alright," he said.

Amelia turned to the guard. "I'm sorry we got so upset," she said. "You were doing your job."

"Thank you, my Lady." The guard bowed his head before heading to Aidan's house.

Amelia and Aidan ran to the manor. When they got to the library, Annabel was sitting on the couch with Geoffrey, and her brother was standing in the window.

"The guards are searching our house!" cried Aidan. "Someone broke in?!" He crouched in front of her. "Are you alright?"

She brushed his hair off his forehead. "I'm alright now, thank you."

He looked at his father. "What happened?"

"She saw someone standing in the hall in front of our bedrooms," he said. He didn't want to tell his son that the intruder was standing in front of HIS door.

"Did you get a good look?" asked Amelia.

"She saw his eyes," Geoffrey answered. He didn't

want to force Annabel to tell the story again. "They were…"

"What?" asked Aidan.

"They were black."

Aidan felt lightheaded. That was exactly how the old man described his eyes earlier in the day. What was the connection? Should he tell them the story? He worried what they would say if they knew. And he didn't know anything other than what the old man blabbered about. No, it wasn't worth the risk to say anything just yet.

Amelia walked over to her brother who was still leaning out the window. He had been unusually quiet. "What's going on?" she asked.

Lord Barton pushed himself up from the sill and slowly turned around. "When she saw him, he vanished in thunder and a flash of light."

"He just disappeared?" asked Aidan.

Amelia put a finger over her lips. She paused to think. "The first noise and light was his arrival. The second was his departure."

Lord Barton nodded. "It could only mean black magic."

"Can't any magician transport himself?" asked Geoffrey.

"It takes great energy," said Lord Barton.

"So much so, that it can rarely be done like this except by a very powerful magician," added Amelia.

"And the eyes," said Lord Barton. "They're the eyes of a man possessed." He lowered his head. "It's a tell-tell sign." He remembered his early apprenticeship. His father took great pains to teach him how to recognize the dark arts. Fire in the eyes is a sign that a magician with great powers was consumed with evil.

Amelia turned. "But father always told me that black magic turned people's eyes red, like blood. Annabel said his eyes were solid black. I don't get it."

"They're not normal," said Lord Barton. "I think father meant that anything like this, whether black or red, is a sign. Druck may have reached a level that no one else has."

Aidan rubbed both of his eyes hard with the palms of his hands. There was a lot to be concerned about. He couldn't get the old man out of his head. The words, *Your eyes were black, Your eyes were black, Your eyes were black* ringed in his ears. He felt like he was going mad. And what if it was Druck? "Why would Druck be in OUR house? I mean, what do we have that he wants?"

"I don't know," said Lord Barton while. "He probably thought Lord Nilet was staying with you. You are healers you know."

What he said did make sense. He was probably looking for the old magician.

"Has anyone checked on him?" asked Amelia.

"Karl's been with him all evening," said her brother. "He's the same."

Aidan felt light-headed, so he plopped down in a chair and rubbed his temples. "This is too much," he said. He had to get it off his chest. "First of all, I had to deal with this old man ranting and raving about magic earlier today, then all this stuff about searching for some mysterious hermit, and now some evil magician is looking through my house. What's next?" He threw his hands in the air.

"Some old man was talking to you about magic?" asked Geoffrey.

"I didn't put any thought into it," said Aidan. He waved his hand through the air as if he had brushed it aside. "I'd given him a little too much Parthworm. He didn't know what he was talking about."

"What did he say?" asked Geoffrey. "You never know if something is related, even if only by fate."

Aidan bit his lip. He was tired of listening to his father keep on and on about fate. "You keep turning everything back to fate. Can't it be that the man was simply over-medicated?" He'd never talked back to his father before, and he wouldn't look him in the eye. But, he meant what he said. Everything wasn't a product of fate, and he wasn't going to let anyone take it any further. He decided not to tell them anymore, especially the part about the black eyes. But it kept eating at him.

Lord Barton shook his head. He didn't want this to turn into an argument. Everyone's nerves were worn thin, and there was no need to force Aidan to talk about. He didn't see the connection anyway. "Let's just go with what we know," he said. "Lord Nilet's unresponsive. Three of the Emperor's best men were killed. Druck, or one of his magicians, shows up in your house."

"It only means that he wants Lord Nilet," said Amelia.

"They're all an act of war!" cried Lord Barton. He was clearly frustrated. "Heshire is the front line!"

Amelia moved close to Aidan and put her hand on his shoulder. "We should wait for Griswold to return with news from Tarsus."

"Wait three weeks? What if we have only one? You can see that he is not afraid to cross the border. What if he comes with an army the next time?"

"And what if there's not a 'next time?'" asked Amelia. "Look at it from his point of view. Our most powerful magician and three armed guards were in his castle. What if THEY crossed the line? Maybe he's after what's his!"

Geoffrey stood. "Why don't you consult your uncle about the matter? He can be reached in a few days."

"He's useless," said Lord Barton.

"He's right," agreed Amelia. "He would run at the first sight of trouble. His advice would be to leave for the north and not return until things have settled down."

"Isn't there another magician you could trust?"

Lord Barton shook his head. "No. Other than Griswold, I know few magicians, and the ones I know are too afraid to make the wrong move...for political purposes. They would never act without the Emperor's order."

"Maybe we should follow suit," said Aidan.

"Lord Nilet may not have that long," said Geoffrey. "His condition grows worse by the day. If he has important information to share, then we need to break the spell before it's too late."

"And another thing...my family was placed here by Leopold the First himself," said Lord Barton. "We were given the mission to protect this border. He saw the need to have someone here who was not concerned with Tarsus politics, and in his infinite wisdom, he must have known that we'd be faced with similar circumstances one day." He pulled Amelia's hand off Aidan's chest. "You, of all people dear sister, should know this."

She closed her eyes and sighed. Her brother was right. Her father beat it into their heads since they were children. They had a purpose for being so far from civilization, and he was proud to serve Gornia in that capacity. She knew her father would have wanted to be here during this difficult time. Doing the right thing would make him proud. "I want to speak to Aidan alone," she said.

Aidan lifted his head, and he slowly stood. "What's going on?"

"I want to talk to you about all of this." She looked at her brother.

"Alright. Where do you want to go?"

"Let's go to the fountain."

The guards had just finished searching the house and were leaving when the two walked out of the manor. Aidan heard one of them say that the old maid probably had too much to drink. They all laughed as they walked back to their barracks. He lunged forward to give them a piece of his mind, but Amelia grabbed his arm and pulled him back. "Let them be," she said. "They don't need to know anything."

"They don't need to talk about Annabel like that either."

"It doesn't mean anything," she said. "They're soldiers. They talk bad about everyone."

"Not about you or your brother."

"What makes you think that?" she asked. "When I was a little girl, I snuck into the stables and saw my father arguing with one of them. Father was furious about something, and when he left, two other guards came into the stable. They must have been listening from outside because they really let my father have it. They said everything in the world about him...none of it true." She ran her fingers through Aidan's hair and smiled. "I wanted to go out there and give them a piece of my mind, but a hand pulled me back. When I turned around, I saw my father, and realized that he'd heard everything too. I asked him if he was going to do something about it, and he said 'no.' He told me they were human too, and they needed a release every now and then because they had stressful jobs. Words, he said, meant nothing. It was action that made a person worthy."

They sat on the edge of the fountain and looked into the sky. "Alright," said Aidan. "I won't say anything to them."

"Did you hear the last thing I said?" asked Amelia.

"What? About words and action?"

"Yes."

"Yes," he replied. "I heard it. What are you getting at?"

"What my brother said in there was true. Our family was put here for a purpose, and it makes sense that we at least consider what they want to do."

Aidan cupped Amelia's face with his hands and stared deeply into her eyes. He knew he had to let her know how he felt, and he didn't care if it was the wrong time to do it. After they'd almost kissed at the canal, he was more confident that she felt the same about him. "Listen, I love you with all my heart... more than anything else in the world..."

She grabbed his wrist and smiled. "I love you

too," she said. "I've always loved you."

His heart melted. He leaned down and pressed his lips to her lips, and they embraced in a long, deep kiss. When they came up for air, Amelia laid her face on his neck and kissed him as he held her. "That was nice," she said.

Aidan was finally relieved. She loved him. She'd always loved him. He regretted waiting so long to tell her how he felt.

She looked at him after laying in his arms for a few minutes. "Now, what were you going to say?"

"I, ah...I was going to say that I'd go along with whatever you decided." He didn't want to tell her what he was really going to say. It didn't matter anymore anyway. Now that they'd confessed their love with one another, he'd follow her to the end of the earth if he had to. And if it meant going on some walk through the mountains to look for someone who didn't exist, then he'd play along as long as he had to.

"Do you see my point?" she asked.

"Action," he said. "We need to take action."

"Are you two love birds done talking?"

Lord Barton looked at them from the library window.

"How long have you been looking at us?" asked Amelia.

"Long enough," said her brother. "I hate to interrupt you from your...conversation...but come back in as soon as you're finished."

"We'll be up in a second. Now give us some privacy or I'll try to light another candle," she yelled.

His eyes grew wide. "Don't even think about it." He moved back inside, closing the curtains behind him.

Aidan ran his fingers through her silky hair, moving from her forehead to the back of her neck. "You are the most beautiful woman in the world."

She laughed. "Stop it. You're making me blush." She paused and smiled. "Well, keep going!"

"I...I don't know why I waited this long to tell you."

"You were scared you'd ruin our friendship," she said. "I know because I felt the same way."

"Would you be happy with me? I mean, you're a magician, and I'm just a healer. Can it work?"

She pushed him softly on the chest. "Of course we can. It's not breaking the code of conduct. It's done quite often."

"What if we marry and have children? What will they be?"

"Healers, silly. The power always falls to the man's side. Hasn't your father taught you anything?"

"No. He hasn't said a word."

"Perhaps he thought it best for you to learn on your own then."

Aidan was still concerned. This was a touchy subject for him, and he thought it would be an issue for her. All magicians want their children to follow suit, he reasoned. "Don't you want your children to have the same abilities as you?"

"Well, it would be nice, but my brother will continue our bloodline, so it really doesn't bother me." She pulled him closer. At the moment their lips touched, she whispered, "The truth is, I have to follow my heart, and my heart tells me you're the only one for me." She kissed him softly, flattening her warm lips across his.

"I feel the same way," he muttered.

She stood. "As much as I don't want to leave, we should be getting up there soon. They're waiting for an answer."

Chapter 13

Lord Griswold trotted into Werth with his two guards at his side. They didn't make it as fast as he'd promised Lord Barton, but he was exhausted from the journey nonetheless, and he knew the horses and his men needed a long rest, so he decided they would stay at least an extra day or more before leaving for Tarsus. It all depended upon how much entertainment he could get at the inn. He was, after all, a single man, and single men had their needs. And until he married, he would explore all of the options at his disposal. He might enjoy them after he had a wife as well, he thought. It just depended upon how good she was to him.

He wasn't in a quick hurry to marry, though. It was a burdensome prospect altogether. After all, he had a prosperous shire to manage, and he was still getting it under control. Conflicts between grape growers, wine makers, and the middle men who bought and sold wine were enough of a headache.

He felt like he had the prospect covered though because he was certain that his good friend Barton would offer his younger sister's hand in marriage in a few years. She was still a little young, but her beauty caught his eye the first time they met, and he wanted her. It would be the perfect arrangement, he concluded. They shared a border, and the marriage would solidify an already strong bond. He could care less about Heshire. It was a dust bowl as far as he was concerned, but to marry a gorgeous magician who came from a good bloodline…it would be the perfect way to satisfy his ambition!

And that's why he was headed to Tarsus. He didn't give a damn about Lord Nilet or Druck. Barton was overreacting in his opinion. It was all just a huge misunderstanding anyway. But leaving for Tarsus got him closer to the three things he cared most about – having fun, making Barton feel obligated to him, and making acquaintances with high ranking officials at the Emperor's court. It was going to be a good month for him, and he was going to milk it for as long as he could without making his friend suspicious.

Werth was a frontier city between the capital and the southern border. Unlike most shires in Gornia, Werth was not controlled by a magician. It was all part of an experiment conducted by Leopold II who wanted to see how people could manage their own affairs without the intervention of a magician's hand. As a result, people of all types flocked to the sleepy hamlet, and over the past twenty years, it had grown into the second largest city in Gornia.

Most people were there to make money. The Emperor forgave all taxes from local commerce, and merchants built stores on its expanding streets. Anything a person wanted could be found here, including gold, silver, medicinal herbs, fresh exotic food, spices, and prostitutes. Lord Griswold was especially appreciative of the prostitutes because they were the most beautiful women in all of Gornia. He had his first prostitute here when he was a young apprentice. She was an older woman, but that's all he could afford at the time. Now, for five pieces of silver, he could get two pretty women for the whole evening.

The Werth Inn was the best inn to stay at in town.

It was expensive but worth it, and he didn't mind spending a few gold pieces for the best accommodations for himself. His guards, however, would stay on the other side of town in the barracks if there was room. If not, there were always the stables. He would not pay for their comfort because it was beneath him, and he felt that it wasn't good to soften the hearts of soldiers.

The lobby of the inn bustled with activity. Wealthy businessmen, magicians of all ranks and file, and merchants selling trinkets out of wooden boxes milled around a seated waiting area in front of the desk. He pushed his way through the crowd eager to get a room and a bath before filling his stomach with the finest food and wine the inn's tavern offered. The last time he was here, he didn't leave the confines of the inn, and he fully expected this stay to be the same.

"How may I help you?" asked the clerk. Although he could tell that Griswold was a magician, rank and file meant nothing in Werth, so titles were disposed of rather quickly.

"I'd like a room," said Griswold. "A good room with a quiet view."

The clerk thumbed through a book on his desk and pointed at an empty block on the second page. "Third floor, room 309," he said. "It's on the end facing the alley. It should be quite quiet."

"Sounds good to me. What's the price?"

"Eight pieces of gold," said the clerk rather smugly.

"Eight pieces of gold?!" replied Griswold as he reached into his leather pouch. "I was here no more than six months ago, and it was only five pieces of gold."

"Our prices went up last week," the clerk explained. "We've been rather busy, you know."

Griswold threw twenty four pieces of gold on the desk. "Put me down for three nights to start." He looked around the room at the crowd. "What's going on?"

"You don't know?" asked the clerk. He laughed as he placed a line through room 309's block on the next three pages in his book.

"No, I don't know. Why don't you enlighten me." Griswold was becoming inpatient with this pompous desk servant.

"The Emperor's convening the Council next week. Everyone from all of Gornia is heading to Tarsus to hear the news."

"What news?"

The clerk looked at him. "Do you live in the Netherlands?"

"Don't worry about where I live, just tell me what news!" demanded Griswold.

The clerk leaned forward and whispered. "Well, no one really knows, but certain people have passed through here over the past week, and the word on the street is that he's signing an alliance with Druck, the new Emperor of Sarcus."

"An alliance with Sarcus?" replied Griswold. This was news. "Why?"

"A hundred years of peace and stability...Gornia and Sarcus will both prosper if the treaty is nullified. And the only way to nullify the treaty is to form an alliance."

Griswold leaned against the desk and shook his

head. Then why was Lord Nilet chased out of Sarcus?. "Have you heard any news of Lord Nilet?"

"Oh yes," whispered the clerk delightfully. "A Sarcugian delegation stayed here just two weeks ago, and I heard them tell Portok…"

"Who is Portok?" interrupted Griswold.

"The Emperor's new advocate. Where have you been the past month?"

Griswold shook his head in disdain. "Why has Lord Nilet been replaced?"

"Like I said," whispered the clerk. "I overheard them telling Portok that the Emperor shouldn't worry." He leaned over the desk a little more and cupped his hand over his mouth. "They said they would take care of Nilet."

"What did he do to them?"

"I don't know for sure, but I heard he tried to kill Druck while on a peace mission for the Emperor. No one's seen him since." He stood straight and closed his book. "Serves the old man right for trying to prevent progress. He's still living in the past."

Griswold smiled. This made perfect sense. No wonder Druck was after the master magician. He grabbed his key from the clerk and headed up the stairs to his room. "I might enjoy this trip longer than I thought," he said to himself.

The tavern was more crowded than usual, and Griswold was forced to take a seat at a small table beside the kitchen door. He wasn't happy about it at all, but there were a lot of people waiting to get in.

He ordered his usual fare – roasted duck, potatoes, and fresh greens, as well as a glass of the finest Sherford wine which was conveniently purchased from his own vineyards. It always pleased him to see his own wine served in such a fine establishment, and he was quick to tell anyone to try that "fabulous wine from the south of Gornia." It was cheap advertisement, after all, and it kept the profits rolling in.

While he sipped his wine, he noticed a tall man with the most fabulous gold cloak walk into the room. He had the darkest black hair he'd ever seen. His olive skin meant that he wasn't from any of the northern provinces, but he didn't look like a southern Gornian either. Must be from Sarcus, he thought, even though he wouldn't know a Sarcugian when he saw one. The man talked to the tavern's host and was pointing at the few empty tables in the room, looking angrier with each passing second. Lord Griswold noted the man's hands – jeweled rings on almost every finger, and his cloak's clasp had a massive green emerald surrounded by gold. This was a man he needed to know. He stood and gestured for the man to join him. He stared at Griswold oddly at first, but after a few more seconds of arguing, he reluctantly waved and walked towards the table.

"May I help you?" asked the man.

"Would you care to dine with me?" asked Griswold. "I see you are having difficulty finding a table."

The man looked at the host. "Oh, that peasant," he said. "He'll pay for his arrogance. I reserved a table earlier this afternoon, and he says he has no record of it."

Griswold stuck out his hand. "I'm Griswold of

Sherford."

The man stuck out a limp hand as if he expected Griswold to kiss his rings. "Lord Bline," he said.

Griswold grabbed Bline's hand and shook it softly. Bline, in return, wiped his hand on his trousers. "A pleasure," he said.

"Would you care to join me?" asked Griswold.

"Well, if I am to eat, I suppose I must."

Griswold almost regretted inviting the well-to-do noble to his table. A fine start to my stay, he thought. He hoped, however, that it would be a prosperous meeting nonetheless. This man had money, and Griswold wanted to make friends, no matter how painful it would be. "Please, make yourself comfortable."

Bline sat and draped his cloak over the back of the chair. "And where are you from again?" he asked.

"Sherford."

"Where in the world is Sherford?" asked Bline smugly.

"It's almost directly south of here on the border with Sarcus."

"Oh, my sakes," said Bline. "I do believe I've been there once before. Would it be that dreadful village amidst all those vineyards?"

Griswold shook his head. Dreadful, he thought? "Inherited from my uncle," he replied. "I'd prefer to live in Tarsus."

"Tarsus is a fine city."

"Where are you from?" asked Griswold.

"Everywhere," said Bline. "I really don't call any place home."

"Alright...then where were you born?"

Bline smirked. "Tarsus."

"And what is it that you do that takes you all over the place?"

"I serve the Emperor."

This peaked Griswold's interest. What a fortunate meeting, he thought. "In what capacity?"

"In any capacity he requires."

Griswold shook his head. He wasn't getting anywhere with this fellow, and it was frustrating him. What would he have to do to get him to talk? He thought for a second and came up with the perfect answer. "Would you care for some wine? It's the finest wine served here."

"Would it by chance happen to come from your vineyards?"

Griswold smiled. A clever fellow too. "It certainly does."

"Very well, then, I'll give it a try."

The dinner conversation was quite painful for Griswold. It was the same time and time again. He'd ask a question, and Bline would give him a short response with little or no meaning. Griswold got nowhere with the strange fellow except the bill which he reluctantly paid. By the time Bline took the last bite of his cobbler, Griswold stood and excused himself from the table. He promised himself that he'd never invite a stranger to dinner again.

The room was as dark and quiet as was promised by the clerk, but it was the odor that woke him in the middle of the night. He sat up, rubbed his eyes, and slammed his fist into the mattress. "What in the world is that smell?" he asked. At first, he thought it smelled like rotten eggs, but the longer he sniffed, the more he was convinced it was a dead rodent in the wall. He'd smelled rotting animals before at some of the untidy farms around Sherford, and it never failed to turn his stomach. It was one thing to smell the country air, but it was another to have to put up with it in a room that cost eight gold pieces a night.

He slung his feet over the bed and reached for his slippers. He would have to inform the desk clerk of this problem and have it resolved immediately. His slippers weren't where he thought he left them, so he held out his hand to emit a small ball of light. The light floated beside the bed, lighting the room enough so he could see the floor.

"Excellent idea," called a voice from a dark corner of the room.

Griswold jumped backwards and landed against the headboard. "Who's there?!" he demanded.

"Oh, you know me," said the voice.

Griswold listened carefully. The voice sounded familiar, but he couldn't place it. He turned his hand over. The ball of light lifted to the ceiling and grew larger, lighting the entire room. He slowly turned to the corner, and what he saw chilled him to the bone. "Father!"

"It is me." His father walked out of the corner and stood at the foot of the bed.

"But...but..." He couldn't find the words. He grabbed the sides of his head with both hands and leaned against the pillow.

"Dead?" The man let out a haunting laugh that echoed through the room.

"Yes…dead," Griswold said very slowly.

His father shrugged his shoulders. "Well, you didn't come to my funeral, so I thought I'd pay you a visit to ask why."

"I…I was only ten. Your brother said I was too young."

"Nolan? That pompous old fool. He never wanted you to love me."

Griswold was afraid to ask, but he had to know. "Why?"

"He wanted you to love HIM! The son he never had." He laughed. "I suppose he got his wish after all. And look what he made you   an arrogant, pompous magician with just enough power to make good tricks." He pointed at the light above the room as an example.

"It's not my fault. I did the best I could. I'm trying to better myself. I really am."

"Do the two bit whores make you better?! Does wine make you better?! Profits from a dying country shire in the middle of nowhere?!"

"No! They make life tolerable! I have plans!"

His father leaned on the foot of the bed, pressing down the mattress with both of his hands. "The only thing that'll give you power and prestige is to ensure the Emperor knows you."

Griswold sat up and poured himself a glass of water. His hands shook, and water splashed on the bed and floor. "I'd offer you some water but I doubt you'll drink."

"You're right about that," said his father. He put his hand on his son's leg. It was icy cold.

"I've come to warn you."

Lord Griswold didn't know how to respond. It was strange talking to a dead man. Even magicians didn't have the power to conjure spirits of the dead. He never even believed in an afterlife before. "This must be a dream," he mumbled.

"I'm not a figment of your imagination."

"Why have you come then?" shook Griswold. He tried to sip his water, but his hands trembled too much.

"Let's just say that I'm giving you an opportunity to start a much better life – a life you would have had if I lived."

He cupped the glass in both hands and finally drank a sip of water. "What do you have for me?"

"A chance."

"Please stop giving me these short answers and tell me why you're here!" He wanted to get this over with, wake up in the morning, and realize that this was a bad dream.

"If you insist. You have a friend…a Lord Barton in Heshire. Right now, he's plotting against the Emperor and…"

"Plotting against the Emperor? Barton?! He would never do anything like that."

"Oh? He's protecting a fugitive isn't he?"

Griswold thought before he responded. "Lord Nilet came to Heshire under Druck's spell. Barton doesn't know the whole story."

"Oh yes he does! He knows everything, and right now he's planning to break the treaty by sneaking into Sarcus! He plans to take the Sarcugian throne."

"And how in the world do you suppose he'll do that? He's as young as me, and he has no army! I don't believe it."

"There's a powerful magician who lives in the Crokus Mountains who despises Druck and wants to overthrow him. Your friend is looking for him and hopes to use him to take the throne."

"If this is true, why doesn't this powerful magician just defeat Druck on his own?"

"Because he's content, and Barton hopes to persuade him to think about things differently. He's going to use his own sister to seal the relationship."

"Amelia?"

"Yes, the woman you hope to marry!" His father laughed.

"I...I don't believe it."

"You don't WANT to believe it, but it's true. I would never mislead you! My own flesh and blood!"

"But I know Barton better than anyone else..."

"He's played you like a fool, and if you continue with your plans to meet with the Emperor on his behalf, you'll be joining me in the afterlife sooner than later."

Griswold slammed his fist into the pillow. "What would you have me do then?!"

"The Emperor is forming an alliance with Druck. Help the Emperor by stopping this treason and return Lord Nilet to Druck!"

"And what do I get out of it?"

"The Emperor's undying gratitude. With that comes power and wealth beyond your imagination."

Griswold paused for a few seconds. He shook his head and grinned. "You know me, don't you?"

"Like a father."

"So, what do I do?"

"You met a stranger last night...a Lord Bline."

"Yes."

"Your meeting was not accidental. He is a loyal servant to the Emperor. He will help you find the traitors."

"That man couldn't stand me."

"He knows your mission, and he will go with you."

"How?"

"I have seen to it. That's all you need to know."

Griswold sucked on his lower lip. "I'm not sure I'm strong enough to beat Barton."

His father pulled a gold chain off his neck and placed it around his son's head. Hanging from the chain was an amulet with an emerald stone. It looked very similar to the stone he saw on Brine's cloak. "This contains all my power. Consider it the cloak I never had the opportunity to make you. It will help you on your journey."

Griswold held the amulet in his hand and stared deeply into the stone. Tiny flashes of light zigzagged through the stone. When he looked up, his father had gone along with the putrid odor. He fell back onto his pillow and thought about everything his father said. Before he knew it, he was asleep.

It was late in the morning by the time he woke. He lied in bed and stared at the ceiling. "What a dream," he grumbled. He rubbed his eyes and yawned. It felt so real. Too much wine, he reckoned. He pushed up and sat against the pillow. When he moved, something heavy brushed across his chest. It couldn't be the amulet his father had given him in the dream, he thought. That would be impossible! Try as he may, though, he couldn't ignore the sensation, so he slowly looked down. His eyes grew wide. It was the amulet. "It's real!" he shouted. He jumped out of bed with urgency. He had to find Bline immediately. His entire life had changed, and former friends be damned, he was going to make sure he caught the eye of the Emperor.

Chapter 14

Geoffrey and Aidan had one thing to take care of before they left for the Crokus Mountains – they had to deliver a baby. Geoffrey had been taking care of the farmer's wife since her third month with child because she was suffering from painful abdominal cramps, and she was afraid she'd lose the baby. To get her through the full nine months, he massaged her belly with Vantam Oil, a powerful concoction consisting of Vantam Root, hog fat oil, and a touch of Billyseed and Lotus Powder.

Over the past five months, he visited her each week to apply the oil and to make sure she was doing well. It was unusual for him to spend so much time with someone, but he had a special affection for this husband and wife, and he would never tell Aidan why.

There was nothing particularly special about the family as far as Aidan could tell. They lived alone on the northern outskirts of Heshire, isolated from the rest of the farming community by the Taber Forest, a five-legion wide old growth forest of considerable density. Only one small road connected them to civilization, and it was over a four-hour ride on horseback to get there.

Aidan went with his father once. They were an older couple, probably in their middle 40s, which surprised Aidan because he didn't know that women of that age could have children. It was certainly a risky pregnancy, however, especially considering this was her first child. Perhaps his father was interested in the outcome, Aidan thought. Many important lessons could be learned from it.

The husband and wife lived in a typical farm house made of logs cut from thick oak, dirt floors, and simple handmade furniture. There were three rooms in the house – the kitchen, the living area, and a small bedroom. When they arrived, the wife was lying in bed just as Geoffrey prescribed the preceding month. He didn't want to take any chances of her going into labor until he was there, and bed rest was one way of ensuring that. Aidan noticed a small crib in the corner of the room. It looked like it had just been made by her husband's hand, and it was perhaps the finest crib he'd ever seen. Just by looking at the crib, he knew how special this child was to these people, and he had a clue as to why his father paid so much attention to them. Sometimes, he thought, being a healer was as much about the bond of humanity as it was about saving a limb or curing a fever. The two components were intertwined most of the time, but in this particular instance, it was becoming obvious that his father had latched onto a special side of the art.

Geoffrey sat at the edge of the bed and felt her stomach. "And how have you been feeling, Tessera?" The dark circles under her eyes and the yellowish tone of her skin told him everything he needed to know, but he wanted to hear it from her lips.

"Tired...weak," she mumbled. "It's been a tough week."

"She's still getting sick," said her husband, Daylon. "Is that normal?" He had farmed this land for over twenty years by himself and ten more before that with his father. He knew how to birth a calf and take care of a pregnant mare, but when it came to his own wife, he was completely helpless.

Geoffrey spread her eyelids open and looked at the whites of her eyes, and he felt the back of her neck. "Sometimes the sickness doesn't stop until the end, especially with the first child. I don't think there's any need to worry." He placed both hands on her belly and pushed gently. "The baby's ready," he said.

"How do you know?" asked Tessera. "My water has not broke."

Geoffrey smiled. "The baby is low. That means it's ready to see you."

Daylon knew from experience with his livestock that it could take days before she gave birth. "Will you be able to come back to deliver the baby?"

Geoffrey grabbed a pouch from his bag and opened it slowly. "Unfortunately, we will be leaving Heshire tomorrow, and I don't know when we'll return." He pulled a long metal rod from the pouch and held it over a candle flame to sear it.

"What do we do? He can't deliver it," Tessera said of her husband. "You've been with us the whole time."

Geoffrey smiled. "I didn't say that I wouldn't birth the baby. I'm just not going to wait for it to come on its own."

Tessera and Daylon looked at each other in confusion.

"Don't worry. You're due to give birth any day now. The baby is ready, and you're ready. We're just going to help it along."

"Is this natural?" asked Daylon.

"Certainly," said Geoffrey. "I wouldn't do it if it

wasn't. There's no magic in delivering a baby." He chuckled. "If it were that easy, they wouldn't call it labor, would they?"

Geoffrey took the rod and handed it to Aidan. "Here, I want you to do it."

Daylon's eyes grew wide. An apprentice?" "Uh… shouldn't you do it? I mean…since you are the one who's been seeing her." One look in Tessera's eyes told him that she was nervous about it too.

"Nonsense. Aidan is perfectly capable of birthing a baby. He's done it many times."

Aidan took the rod and stepped towards the end of the bed. His father was right – he'd delivered many babies, but he'd never induced one. He knew all about the procedure, but actually doing it for the first time was a little nerve-racking. In all fairness, though, directed supervision was the only way for a healer to gain knowledge and experience.

"Slide towards me, please," he told Tessera. "And take off your undergarments."

What choice did she have? She looked at Daylon silently for assurance, and he reluctantly nodded. She had to trust Geoffrey's opinion. So, she positioned herself on the bed as he asked, and Daylon moved the pillows underneath her head. She pulled up her nightgown, slid her underwear off, and spread her legs wide.

Aidan looked at Daylon. "Stay right there," he said. "I might need you to hold her legs when the baby comes.

Daylon nodded his head and watched as Aidan knelt to the floor and.

Aidan pulled out a jar of boiled hog's fat and

smeared his right hand with the slimy jelly. He then inserted his right hand slowly into her vagina.

Tessera's hips lurched back as she felt the pressure of his hand inside her.

"What's he doing?" Daylon asked Geoffrey.

"He's making sure her hips have spread enough," said Geoffrey. "He's also checking the membrane to make sure it's thinned."

Aidan pulled his hand out and wiped his hand with a clean cloth. "She's ready."

Geoffrey stood back and observed Aidan as he inserted the rod slowly into her vagina. With one effortless push, the membrane broke and a trickle of water dripped onto the bed. In a few seconds, the trickle turned into a steady stream as several cups of the sticky fluid came out.

Tessera lurched up as her stomach muscles contracted. "It hurts!" she said.

"I want you to push when you feel your stomach tighten," said Aidan. "Push with all your might." He reached into the bag and pulled out a jar of concentrated Vantam Oil. When diluted, the oil prohibits contractions early in pregnancy, but when it's concentrated, it has the opposite effect and forces contractions. He poured the oil over her belly and rubbed it in thoroughly before standing up. "The baby will come soon," he said.

Geoffrey patted his son on the shoulder. "You're doing great!"

"Tell me that when the baby's out," whispered Aidan. He watched as Daylon wiped Tessera's head with a wet cloth. "These people mean a lot to you, don't they?"

"I feel for them," said his father. "They've been trying to have a baby for a long time, and when they thought there was no chance, she became pregnant. I have a connection with that."

"How so?"

Geoffrey looked into Aidan's eyes. "I just do." He turned and walked out the bedroom. "I'm going to draw some fresh water from the well."

Tessera screamed. "Ah! It's coming!"

Aidan whirled around and felt her belly. The baby had moved quicker than expected and was lodged at the base of her hips. He pushed gently near her belly button, and then he started pushing harder and harder all around her lower belly.

"What's the matter?" Daylon didn't like the look in the boy's eyes.

"The baby's turned," Aidan said. Sweat started pouring from his forehead. "Father!" he shouted

Geoffrey was outside at the well and couldn't hear his son.

"Do you want me to get him?!" asked Daylon. His voice was filled with concern.

"There's no time! If I don't move it now, it won't make it!"

"I've repositioned foals many times!" cried Daylon. "What's the matter?!"

"The cord is wrapped around its neck!" Aidan exclaimed.

Daylon's heart sank. "Then do something!"

Tesseara's hips lurched high off the bed as she twisted back and forth. She felt like she was being pulled apart.

Aidan quickly rubbed his hand with fat. He

shoved it in her vagina and grabbed the baby's foot. "I've got to turn the baby before I try to move the cord!" As hard as he tried, he couldn't get the baby's leg back into the womb. It pushed against his every attempt. After several seconds, he pulled his hand out. "Dammit!" he yelled.

"Hurry!" shouted Daylon. "Time's running out!"

Aidan jumped up and felt the woman's belly once again. He could feel the baby's head and the large lump around its neck. He was panicking, and his father was nowhere to be found. If he lost this baby, he'd never forgive himself. His heart pounded in his chest. He started to feel warm and lightheaded.

Daylon looked at Aidan and almost passed out in fear. The boy's eyes were turning dark. A swirl of black turned rapidly like a tornado until his entire eyeballs looked like pieces of coal. He watched in horror as Aidan calmly reached down and stuck both hands through his wife's belly. Sparks of light flickered on her skin as he pulled and turned his arms inside her. Aidan smiled as if he could see the baby, but he didn't say a word as he worked. After a few seconds, a sheet of light glowed across her abdomen as Aidan pulled the baby through her stomach and handed it to her father. The umbilical cord stuck out through his wife's belly button. Aidan touched the cord with his finger and severed it.

Tessera passed out as soon as Aidan put his arms into her stomach, but Daylon hadn't even noticed. He was too focused on the miracle he'd just witnessed. He looked at his wife's belly, and there was no sign of blood or the cord. He couldn't tell that anything had been done to her.

Aidan handed the baby to Daylon, closed his eyes, and fell to the floor.

An hour went by before Aidan regained consciousness. Geoffrey and Daylon had laid him across the kitchen table, and when he rolled over, he fell to floor. Geoffrey ran out of the bedroom and helped him to his feet. "Are you alright?" he asked as he examined Aidan's eyes.

"What happened?" Aidan mumbled. He ran his fingers through his hair and concentrated. His eyes opened wide, and he pushed past his father. "The baby!"

Geoffrey grabbed his sleeve. "They're sleeping."

Aidan pulled against his father's grasp. "It's in breach. I've got to reposition it!"

"You mean 'him,'" said his father. "Everything's alright. The baby's doing fine."

Aidan looked into the bedroom and saw that Tessera was asleep. He leaned into the room and saw the baby in the crib. "You saved it!" he exclaimed.

Geoffrey shook his head. "No. You did." He put his hand across his son's shoulders and pulled him close. "It was all you."

Aidan looked at his father in disbelief. "I did? I don't remember a thing."

"It was the most incredible thing I've ever seen in my life!" exclaimed Daylon. "Your eyes…"

Geoffrey raised his hand to silence Daylon. "He saved little Aidan, so let's just leave it at that." Geoffrey saw the whole thing from the back of the room.

By the time he returned with the water, Aidan's arms were sticking into Tessera's belly. Geoffrey was so stunned that he couldn't move, and before he knew it, Aidan had handed the baby to Daylon and collapsed. He knew that Aidan had unknowingly used magic to save the mother and baby, but he didn't know how that was possible. And since Aidan was seemingly unaware of what he did, he didn't want to make a scene of it until he was able to do some research into his son's apparent powers. There were just too many questions left unanswered, and his experience told him that he needed to get more information before asking questions, especially when it concerned something like this.

Aidan sat down on the kitchen chair. "You named the baby Aidan?" he asked.

Daylon proudly walked toward the young healer. "We sure did. It was Tessera's idea. It was the least we could do."

Aidan put his hand over his mouth. "I...I don't remember doing anything except panicking."

Daylon glanced at Geoffrey before he spoke and nodded his head. "You did a great job. Thank you." He patted Aidan on the back before returning to the bedroom.

"Do you feel well enough to ride?" asked Geoffrey. "We need to get back. We're meeting Lord Barton and Amelia for dinner again."

"Yea...I'm fine. I just wish I knew what I did."

"It'll come to you in time, don't worry," said Geoffrey. He grabbed the bag and headed for the front door.

Aidan peeked into the bedroom one more time

to make sure the baby was doing fine. Daylon was sitting beside the crib staring into the baby's eyes. Little Aidan was doing well. Aidan smiled. It was a beautiful sight. He turned around slowly and walked away. Although more confused than anything, he was relieved that the ending was as happy as it was.

Chapter 15

Amelia ran out the front door as soon as she saw Aidan and Geoffrey head down the street towards the stables. She'd been reading by the window for a few hours while she waited for them, and had gotten worried after they didn't show up when Geoffrey said they would. All sorts of scenarios raced through her mind during those long two hours, the biggest of which was that Druck had followed them into the forest and had taken them prisoner or killed them.

She ran to Aidan and threw her arms around his neck as soon as he dismounted. "I'm so happy you're back!" she said. She gave him a kiss and squeezed him tightly.

Geoffrey dismounted his horse and went into the stable without saying a word.

"What's wrong with him?" asked Amelia. "Is he upset about us?"

Aidan watched his father walk away. "I don't think it has anything to do with that. I'm sure he's happy for us."

Amelia smiled and pulled Aidan close. "Then what's the matter?"

"I really don't know. He wasn't upset about anything that I'm aware of, but he didn't talk much on the way back either." Aidan knew it had something to do with his blackout, but he didn't want to worry Amelia about it. Deep down, though, he worried that his father was concerned about his ability to be a good healer. After all, blacking out during a crisis was not a good thing, even if things worked out well. He hoped his father would open up to him in the near future to explain what had happened.

Amelia grabbed Aidan's arm and pulled him towards the manor. "The guard's will take care of your horse. Let's go inside. I have a surprise for you!"

Aidan followed her into the sitting room. She sat him down and told him to close his eyes. Then she left the room. He sat there for a couple of minutes, occasionally peeking to see where she was.

"I see you," she bellowed. "Keep your eyes closed."

She's nowhere in sight, he thought. How can she see me? He chuckled. Women have eyes in the back of their head, he thought, and since she was a magician, she probably did.

"Tada!"

He sat still and kept his eyes closed.

"You can open your eyes now," she said.

"I was waiting for you to tell me," he said. "You seem to know when I'm cheating." When he opened his eyes, she handed him a crimson cloak. "It's beautiful," he said. "You made it?" He reached out and felt the heavy silk fabric.

"My brother helped me, but, yes, I did most of the work."

"Is it the cloak you'll wear when you finish with your uncle?"

"You're not much of a healer, are you?" she joked.

Aidan was confused. "I guess not."

"It's yours, silly. Now stand up so I can put it around your neck."

Aidan slowly stood. "I'm not a magician, though. How can I…"

"Healers generally wear a cloak, so you need one too."

"But I'm not a healer. I'm still an apprentice."

"My brother talked to your father about it last night, and he said you were ready for it."

"But he doesn't wear one," said Aidan. He was grateful for the gift, but he worried that it was inappropriate.

"He never has, and I have never been able to figure that out about him. All the other healers do. It's a symbol of your position."

She clasped the gold chain and walked him to the mirror on the other side of the room. "What do you think?"

The cloak fit him well. He turned around to look in the mirror. "It's beautiful. My father never told me about healer's cloaks. What does it mean?"

"Well, healer's always wear crimson. But this cloak is more special than that because it was made by magic, so you've got a special advantage that most other healer's don't have."

"What?"

"All the healing magic that you possess is contained in the fabric of the cloak."

"You mean, like a magician's cloak?"

"Yes, just like it, except yours contains the power to heal."

"So I don't need the medallion and healing stone?"

"Nope."

Aidan whirled around in his new cloak and smiled. "That's amazing," he said. "And my father approved?"

"He told my brother you were ready to learn healing magic, so you'd need it anyway."

Aidan's eyes lit up. "I can't believe you did this for me! Thank you!" He reached down and gave her a deep kiss. "I love you."

"You're welcome." She kissed him on the cheek and hugged him tightly. "I love you too."

And she did. So much so that she ached inside. She had loved him since they were children, and as she got older, she just knew he was the one for her.

Perhaps her father wouldn't have approved. She'd never know. But her brother did. After all, it was up to him to carry on the bloodline anyway. He knew Aidan and his father, and he knew they were good people who cared for others. No one else could care for her like Aidan, and he knew it. And the one time he dared mention Griswold, she threw such a fit that he promised to never mention the arrangement again. Griswold wasn't right for her anyway. He knew it, and he wouldn't try to force the issue. No, Aidan was right for her.

Geoffrey spent the remainder of the afternoon in his library with the doors closed. He pulled almost every book off the shelves thumbing from one page to the next looking for any information he could find about Aidan's sudden ability. As far as he knew, healer's couldn't do what he saw his son do that afternoon, and he was hoping he'd find something…anything… that would tell him otherwise. The black eyes bothered him most because they were the same as the mysterious intruder. He refused to believe that Aidan had anything to do with black magic, so there had to be another answer.

If he couldn't find anything, he knew he would have to talk to Lord Barton about it, and that would only mean telling Aidan everything, and he wasn't ready for that. He'd kept the secret for twenty-two years now, and he wasn't about to break the promise he made his wife so many years before unless he absolutely had to.

By the time Aidan returned to get ready for dinner, the library was a disaster. The couch was stacked with books, scrolls were piled on chairs, and stray papers were strewn across the floor.

"Dad!" yelled Aidan as he opened the front door. "Dad!"

Geoffrey carefully stepped over the paper, cracked the door, and stuck his head into the hall. "Yes?"

Aidan walked briskly towards him, his new cloak fluttering in the breeze. "You knew about this, and you didn't tell me?!" He grinned from ear to ear.

Geoffrey looked at his son's new cloak. "You're handsome."

"Why didn't you tell me earlier?"

Geoffrey smiled for the first time since they left the farmhouse. "Amelia threatened to turn me into a chicken if I did."

"I didn't think I was ready. It really took me by surprise."

Geoffrey looked blankly at the hall wall. "Well you are ready."

"Why didn't you tell me about healer's cloaks before? You don't wear one."

"I've never cared too much for status. It makes no

difference to me, but since you're probably going to marry into their family, it's right for you."

Aidan nodded. "I understand. It also contains my healing magic. Did you say it was alright?"

"Well, it will when the time's right."

Geoffrey was acting a little too reserved. "Is everything alright?" he asked.

Geoffrey looked at the floor and closed his eyes. "Everything's fine. Don't worry about it. Dinner is in an hour, so you'd better get ready." He pulled his head back and closed the door softly.

Aidan reached for the doorknob and almost turned it, but he realized his father needed some time alone, so he let go and slowly walked away.

Geoffrey leaned back against the door and rubbed his face. "I'm trying, honey. I'm really trying."

Dinner wasn't as good as it was the night before. Because of everything that happened, Geoffrey gave Annabel some time off so she could visit her sister in Sherford. She gladly accepted and took off early in the morning before they left. Geoffrey hoped she would return, but he couldn't blame her if she didn't.

After they finished eating, the four returned to the library where Lord Barton had laid out maps of the Crokus Mountains. Before the war, his grandfather spent several months on a trip through the region and had made those maps from his observations. Roads were plotted, villages were marked, and interesting geographical features such as streams and forests were noted. Lord Barton figured the rugged mountain range had probably remained unchanged over time. Very few people went through the mountains except locals whose families had lived there for generations, so the maps would probably be useful.

Lord Barton pointed at the map. "We should cross the Elbe here," he said.

"Why don't we just take the Heshire Road?" asked Amelia.

"Because they're probably watching it," said Lord Barton impatiently. "Several villagers told me they saw the light come from that area. Druck probably has a garrison stationed there. If we cross east of Heshire, we have a better chance of going in undetected."

Amelia nodded.

Geoffrey had been to this part of the Elbe before. It was a good place to cross. He drew his finger up the map. "Looks like there's a small village here." He squinted and pulled the map closer to his face. "Birkstow," he said. "It'll be a good place to start."

Aidan stood behind the three as they looked. He couldn't believe they were actually going to look for this mysterious magician. The idea that such a man existed was beyond his reasoning, and the only reason he agreed to go was to protect Amelia. He hoped she would help him talk the other two out of it, but since her brother had convinced her that it was the right thing to do, he was outnumbered. "So, let me get this right. Our plan is to cross into Sarcus, go to Birkstow, and ask the villagers where this man is, right?"

"Do you have a better plan?" asked Geoffrey. He knew when his son was being sarcastic.

Aidan could tell that he had almost crossed the line by the way his father looked at him. "No. I think it's as good a plan as any," he said. "I was just making sure that's what we are going to do."

"It's a start," said Lord Barton.

"If your father heard of this man, then the locals have certainly heard of him too or at least the legend," said Geoffrey.

"I'm counting on that fact. It's going to be important to listen to the villagers so we can pick up what little facts we can."

"It's also going to be important that we treat them well," said Geoffrey. "I'm sure they haven't had a healer or magician travel through their parts in years, so we need to do as much good for them as we can. Just because they're Sarcugians doesn't mean they support Druck."

"Chances are, they don't," said Lord Barton. "They're too far away from Pilas to matter to him. I've got a feeling that's why the magician healer settled there."

"So you think there's little chance that Druck will have spies there?" asked Aidan.

Lord Barton looked up from the map. "That's always a possibility, so we need to keep a sharp eye for any clues. But there's a greater chance that he has no allies there."

"I wish we knew his name," said Amelia. "It would make it so much easier to find his descendents."

"I'm sure people will know who we're asking about," said Lord Barton. He rolled the maps and put them in a black bag. "Are we settled?"

Everyone nodded.

"Good. We leave at sunrise." He turned to Aidan. "By the way, nice cloak!"

Aidan smiled. "Thank you for helping Amelia make it. I love it!"

"I'm glad you do." He walked to the door and held out his hand. "Amelia and I have some things to work on tonight, so if you'll excuse us…"

Amelia gave Aidan a peck on the lips and leaned into his ear. "We're working on my magic," she whispered. "I'm not looking forward to it."

Aidan smiled and nodded. "Good luck." He kissed her again. "Don't burn the house down," he whispered.

As soon as they left, Lord Barton walked to the fireplace and opened a pair of trap doors hidden beneath a carpet, revealing a set of stone steps that led to his workroom. He flicked his finger through the air, lighting the torches that hung on the wall. "Let's get started."

"Are you sure I'm ready?" she asked.

"As sure as I'll ever be," he echoed from below.

Amelia reluctantly followed her brother. "Shouldn't we check on Lord Nilet first?" she asked.

"Stop stalling. I checked on him before dinner, and Karl is with him right now. If there are any changes in his condition, he'll let us know. Now come on!"

The basement was as large as the first floor of the manor and was totally enclosed with stone. The only light came from torches that lined the walls and some candles on a desk at the back of the room. Amelia had been down here many times with her father but wouldn't stay long because it was such a spooky place. While dry, it was quite cool, and there was nothing to see other than the desk and a bookcase that stood against the wall.

The bookcase contained hundreds of books and scrolls handed down from generation to generation. Essentially, all of the magic they had inherited for over a thousand years. This was a sacred place for the family, and no one could come down here unsupervised. Lord Barton had never invited anyone to see the room, nor did his father.

All of the magic Lord Barton learned was practiced in the confines of these walls for days before he was allowed to practice in the open. The stones themselves were made from the magic of his grandfather's hands, and they absorbed any stray magic before it could be unloosed outside the manor.

Her brother stood in front of the empty fireplace and held his hand out. Three fresh logs appeared on the iron grate. "We're going to start with making fire," he said. He turned towards her. "Since you seem to have problems with that."

Amelia sighed and leaned against the back wall. "This is a waste of time," she said. She closed her eyes and crossed her arms in defiance of his instruction.

"Get over here," he demanded. "We don't have all night."

"What if I don't want to?"

Her brother turned and reached out his hand. "This is the last time I'm going to ask nicely," he said.

She turned her head and didn't say a word.

Lord Barton shook his head. "You're being childish about this. There's nothing to it!"

"I almost burned down the manor last night."

"But I stopped it. You've got to trust me."

Amelia shook her head. "I'd rather wait."

Lord Barton made a fist. A breeze blew through the room, bending the flames of the torches towards the floor. Her feet lifted off the ground, and she floated towards him through the air.

"You're going to force me, aren't you?" she asked as she levitated in front of him.

"You're going to do it," he said. He opened his hand, and she dropped to the floor.

"Easy next time!" she demanded.

He smiled. "Set the logs on fire, and I'll consider it."

She stared at the wood and closed her eyes slowly. I can do this, she thought. All I have to do is concentrate on the logs, and it'll work. I won't set the manor on fire, she reassured herself. After a few seconds, she opened her eyes and pointed her finger at the logs. The tip of her finger glowed red and a small fireball shot out, zigzagged around the fireplace and exploded against the wall, catching the stones on fire. She put her hand over her open mouth and stepped back. Before she could blink, the fire was sucked into the stones and disappeared without leaving singe marks.

"I told you that you couldn't hurt anything," said her brother.

Amelia slapped her thighs. "What is wrong with me?!"

"There's nothing wrong with you. You think I could do it when I first tried?"

She shrugged her shoulders.

"I did the same thing."

"How did you finally get it right?" She'd been trying to make fire for weeks now and couldn't control it.

It was the most frustrating magic she'd ever tried.

"Making fire is tricky and takes a lot of concentration at first. Once you get the hang of it, it's nothing. Look." He reached behind his back and a pointed at the logs. A stream of fire shot from his finger and engulfed the logs. "See?"

"The only thing I see is a show-off," she said. Then she started laughing. "I'm sorry. I didn't mean anything by that."

Lord Barton shook his head and waved his hand at the fire, putting it out immediately. "Listen. Visualize what you want to do and see it happen in your head before you try. Did you see my fire? It wasn't a little fireball was it? Fireballs are difficult to control, so stick to the basics until you practice. Then try fireballs."

"But I remember watching you and father shooting fireballs. I want to be like you."

"I didn't start out with fireballs or any other advanced magic for that matter. You never saw me while I practiced. I was down here for hours each day working on my magic."

Amelia nodded.

"Now, do what I told you."

She pointed her finger, closed her eyes, and concentrated. She saw a stream of fire come out of her finger. She saw the logs catch on fire. She saw herself stopping the stream of fire, and she saw the logs burning. When she opened her eyes to do the magic, she was surprised to see the logs already burning in the fireplace. "Why did you do that?"

"I didn't," he replied. "You did."

She opened her mouth. "I did that?" She couldn't

believe it.

"Of course you did. You were concentrating.
That's what magic is all about. After a while, you'll be
able to do it without thinking so much. And with your
eyes open." He walked towards the steps that led
back to the library. "Now get to work. I've got to get
ready for our journey."

Amelia closed her eyes and pointed her finger
at the fireplace once again. Within a few seconds, a
strong wind blew the fire out. This is the best I've
done in months, she thought. And, for the first time
since she'd come down here, she was thankful her
brother forced her to do it. For the rest of the evening,
she lit the wood and put the fires out until she could
do it with her eyes open.

Chapter 16

Griswold hurried to the lobby and waited for Lord Bline to walk by. He fingered the amulet nervously and stared at it. The whole idea of having more magical power was exciting, and he couldn't wait to leave Werth so he could try it out. Unlike every other province in Gornia, magic was forbidden in Werth. And any magician caught breaking the law was automatically sentenced to one year in the Emperor's prison.

He thought about what his father said about Barton. He still wasn't convinced. Barton wasn't a conspirator, or at least he never appeared to have those intentions. Perhaps Lord Nilet was to blame. Maybe he had Barton under his thumb. His father said he should grab Barton in the Crokus Mountains, but maybe, he thought, he should take Lord Nilet first to see if he could block the spell. This was something he'd have to discuss with Lord Bline

He waited for Lord Bline for over an hour. The desk clerk said there was no "Lord Bline" registered at the inn. He probably registered under another name for the sake of privacy, he reasoned, and he continued to wait until noon when he finally gave up and returned to his room.

By the time he walked through the door, the maid had already put fresh linens on the bed. The room smelled like lemons, a refreshing smell considering the odor that woke him the night before. He threw his cloak on the back of a chair and lied on the bed. The more he thought, the more he determined that he would continue with his original plans until Lord

Bline showed up. Why wait in idle time when he could be having fun?

Griswold was asleep when they knocked on the door. "Just a second," he said. The knocking continued. "I said, just a second!" The last thing he tolerated was impatience on the part of other people, especially the lower class. He rubbed his eyes, dropped his feet to the floor, and slowly walked to the door.

A tall woman leaned into the doorway. She had the darkest hair he'd ever seen, and her crystal blue eyes stood in stark contrast to her olive skin. Her plump breasts pushed hard against a tight corset as she leaned forward to kiss him on the lips. She winked and put her hand against his chest, sliding it down to his groin as she walked in. Behind her was a young brunette with freckles and pale skin. She walked past him, shyly staring at the floor, and stopped behind her older companion.

Griswold smiled. Finally, he thought, the good times begin. He closed the door, faced the two women and stared. An older one and an inexperienced girl, he thought. "Just as I requested," he mumbled.

"You are pleased?" asked the black-haired beauty. She reached back and caressed the young prostitute's face.

"Very much so." His groin immediately came to life when he saw the two touch. "Go ahead and undress." He moved to his bed to watch.

The two women began to unbutton their corsets. The mature woman stared at him with wanting eyes while she slowly let loose each button, gradually showing the fullness of her breasts second by second. He glanced at the other one. She undressed slowly and unsurely, seeming to not enjoy the moment like her friend. But she was obedient nonetheless, and that's all that mattered right now.

After a few long minutes, both women stood naked in front of him. He smiled with nervous enthusiasm. He hadn't had a woman in a few months now, and he would certainly get his money's worth from these two. By the time he was done, he thought, they'll be exhausted and sore.

"What would you like?" asked the older woman.

"Start with each other," he said softly.

The older prostituted turned around and leaned towards the brunette, kissing her softly on the lips. Their mouths opened wide and they closely embraced in a deep kiss. The younger one was a little stiff at first, but as she kissed the taller woman, she loosened up and reached her hand around her friend's back and massaged her bottom. They pulled their lips apart, and the older woman slid down and began to suck her companion's neck. She rubbed the girl's groin with her fingers, dropped slowly to her knees and kissed her inner thigh.

Griswold unbuckled his belt and slid his pants off while he watched the young prostitute enjoy her friend's attention. The girl leaned her head back and moaned while running her fingers through the woman's long dark hair to pull her face deeper into her groin. Her eyes grew wide with excitement as the woman began to lick her softly.

"Come to me," Griswold said. His heart raced,

and his bulging manhood was ready for equal attention from the two.

The tall woman turned and smiled with wet lips.
"Our pleasure," she said. She crawled on her knees
towards the bed and pulled herself slowly to Griswold, raking her hands across his leg as she rose. She
moved methodically onto the bed, licking him across
his thigh until she got to his groin when she pulled
away and lifted her head in ecstasy. He looked to see
her point of pleasure and saw the brunette's face buried deep in her bottom. He grabbed the tall woman's
hand and placed it around his erect member which she
massaged with soft hands while enjoying her friend's
attention.

He reached forward and grabbed the back of
the woman's head, pulling it down to his groin. She
smiled before taking him into her mouth. The pleasure was overwhelming. He threw his head back
on the pillow, and enjoyed her hot, wet mouth while
watching the brunette work on her.

After a few minutes, he was close to finishing this
round of pleasure. He put his hand on her head and
began to push down to make her go faster. At first,
she complied, but as he was nearing completion, she
forced her head against his hand and stopped.

"What are you doing?!" he asked in frustration.
He couldn't believe she stopped at the very end, and
he was throbbing with the need to release. "Finish!"
he demanded.

The woman moved to her knees and looked at
him. Her eyes were now red. She wiped the spit from
her mouth, turned around and struck the brunette in
the head with her hand, knocking her into the back

wall.

Griswold soon forgot about the missed opportunity for final pleasure. He looked toward the wall and saw the young prostitute lying on the floor, her eyes opened by a quick death from a broken neck. He nervously crawled back against the wall and pushed himself against the headboard. "Who are you?! What do you want?!" He reached towards the floor to grab his money bag. "Is it money you're after?" He pulled a few coins from the purse and threw them at her. "Here! Now leave me!"

"I don't need your money," said the woman. She moved off the bed and stood over him. "I need you to stop your foolish games you weak fool!" Her voice grew deeper as she spoke. "You have a mission!" Before he could say a word, her black hair turned brown, and her breasts disappeared. He couldn't believe his eyes when he saw a naked Lord Bline standing in front of him.

"You?" he asked. "You were her?!" His heart thumped in his chest and his head swirled in confusion.

Lord Bline wiped his mouth with the back of his hand and smiled. He closed his eyes as if he were trying to regain his composure, then he moved to the bed, putting a knee beside Lord Griswold's thigh. He leaned forward as if he were about to kiss the confused magician, stopping a few inches from his face to speak. "I am many things to many people," he said softly. He reached down, grabbed Griswold's limp member, and started to massage it.

Griswold tried to turn away, but the powerful magician immobilized him. "Would you like me to finish the job?" asked Lord Bline.

Griswold tried to speak, but he couldn't, and when Lord Bline put his mouth over his groin, he shut his eyes tightly.

"Griswold, what's the matter?" asked a familiar voice. He slowly opened his eyes and was surprised to see Amelia kneeling naked over him. She looked exactly like she did the last time he saw her. Before he knew what happened, she bent down and began to caress him slowly with her mouth, staring into his eyes the entire time. This can't be, he thought. How is he doing this? He tried to resist the temptation, but the thought of Amelia bearing down on him was too much, and he exploded in a few seconds of ecstasy.

When he looked back up, Lord Bline was standing at the foot of the bed dressed as he was the night before. Griswold was light-headed. He leaned over the bed, grabbed his pants, and slid them on. "Why?!" he demanded. His hands were shaking so badly that he couldn't clasp his belt. He threw the ends down in frustration. "Why would you do that to me?!"

Lord Bline smiled. "To show you what you're up against," he said. He turned towards the dead girl at the back of the room. "Pity," he said. "She was such a charming young lady." He pointed his finger at the limp body and turned it in small circles. Red sparks covered her skin until she disappeared in a flash of light.

"How are you able to use magic here?" Griswold asked.

Lord Bline turned. "I'm the Emperor's..." He paused and looked at the ceiling. "Right hand."

"So that gives you the right to trick me, murder an

innocent girl, and use your magic where it's forbidden?"

"Some people are just beyond the law," said Lord Bline as he shrugged his shoulders. "You've got a lot to learn about how things really work in Tarsus." He reached his hand out and spread his fingers. Griswold's amulet lifted off the floor and flew into Lord Bline's hand. "Your father's?" he asked. He stared at the emerald before throwing it to the bed with a smirk. "You'll need it."

Griswold grew with rage and his face turned red as the amulet bounced across the mattress. "I should kill you for what you've done to me!" he shouted. He raised his arm pushed his hand towards Lord Bline. A bright blue ball of electricity shot out of his palm.

Lord Bline raised his hand quickly, deflecting the ball to the wall where it exploded in a thousand blue sparks. The magic blew a hole in the wall between Lord Griswold's room and the next room.

"You cannot harm me," said Lord Bline. "I am too powerful for you my boy. It's not even worth your effort."

"What do you want with me?" demanded Griswold. A defeated calm fell over him as he realized he was no match for this fight.

"Just to show you what you're getting yourself into," said Lord Bline. "Your father came to me too, you know, and he told me to give you a very rude awakening. You don't question the dead, do you?"

"How did you know of Barton's sister? Have you met her?"

"I read your mind," said Lord Bline. He looked at the young magician with a crooked smile. "You are too easy, my friend. You need to strengthen your defenses."

"This was my father's idea?"

Lord Bline nodded his head. "Shaking you up was his idea. How I did it was up to me." He laughed. "It was…rather enjoyable."

Griswold slammed his fist into his leg in frustration. "I waited downstairs for you for several hours! I was willing to go to Sarcus to find Barton! Why did you have to go through with this?!"

"Willing?" Lord Bline moved closer to Griswold. "Willing? Were you not thinking that your father was wrong about your friend? Didn't you come up with the idea of taking Lord Nilet first?" Lord Bline moved within a few inches from Griswold's face. "Was that the plan?! Was that what your father told you to do?! He sees from the Netherworld…a vision that only dead magicians can see…and you ignore his advice?!" He stomped his foot on the floor in anger. "Do you want Gornia and Sarcus to go to war?!"

Griswold leaned back as Lord Bline chastised him. He'd never been spoken to this way before. He bowed his head and softly said, "No."

Lord Bline put his hands on Griswold's shoulders and smiled. "Good. I'm glad to hear it." He turned and walked toward the door. "We leave in an hour." He pointed at the amulet before opening the door. "You've got a few days to acquaint yourself with your father's magic. What you saw today is nothing compared to what's facing you."

After he left, Griswold fell to his knees. He pounded his fists on the floor. "How could you do this to me?!" he yelled. "Why me?!"

Chapter 17

When the old man ruled Sarcus, the castle was adorned with brightly colored silk tapestries made by the best artisans in Pilas. A warm southern breeze blew through the windows, and sunlight lit its halls with a soft, warm glow. The people of the old capital were happy and content, and they had reason to be. They were ruled by a benevolent king bent upon keeping peace in the land so the citizens could finally prosper without fear of reprisal and over-taxation.

Druck's father emerged as king thirty years after the fall of the Council of Magicians during the war with Gornia. He inherited a broken people who were mired in the muck of a two-hundred-year dark age where black magic ruled the land. To the council, the inhabitants of the land were nothing more than a necessary nuisance. When slaves from other lands could not be procured at a reasonable rate, Sarcugian peasants were rounded up, put in the dungeon, and drained of their life force for the sake of more powerful black magic. Hundreds of thousands of these peasants had been killed, and no one could do anything to stop the powerful warlord magicians from imposing their will upon them.

That's why Druck's father drastically changed everything overnight. He knew the people were the key to true power and stability. "Black magic destroys everything in its sight," he would say, and he did everything in his power to abide by the Gornian Treaty to prevent magicians from dabbling in the dark art.

He kept tabs on magicians through a secret police

who had the power to arrest any magician known to be using black magic. This was a successful practice; however, it alienated him from many powerful master magicians who resented being spied upon. Several of these magicians attempted to de-throne him on numerous occasions, but he was always able to garner enough support from those who saw the good he was doing, and he kept the throne until the day he died.

While he was good at watching other magicians, he neglected to observe his own son's behavior. Even though Druck grew up in the splendor of the throne, he was a fatherless child for the most part, raised by an old magician who knew the ways of the council. Under his own nose, the king's worst nightmare was being slowly developed without anyone noticing, not even his secret police.

By the time Druck became a teenager, he was a proficient magician. He hadn't practiced black magic yet, but his mentor had been preparing him mentally for the transition. Under the old teacher's direction, Druck instigated a violent argument with his father which led to his exile to the family's old country estate in the western mountains of Sarcus far from anyone of importance. There, the old magician schooled young Druck in black magic, and for eight years, his prodigy became more powerful than anyone in the land without anyone paying the slightest attention to what was going on.

On the day of his father's death, Druck took his seat on the throne, appearing from thin air in the form of a lightning bolt. By the time the members of the royal court realized what had happened, Druck incinerated them with a simple wave of his hand. That became his particularly favorite form of punishment ever since.

Hundreds of magicians loyal to his father rose against him in the hope that their combined powers would overpower the son's black magic. There was a three-day siege on the castle, but Druck defended himself well, and through the support of his old teacher, he was able to beat back the magicians. He personally hunted each and every one of them over the next year, sending them all to an early death.

Over the next two years, he focused his efforts on re-building his army and fighting small wars with pesky neighbors, and in the process reestablished a war-like state that fed off the fears of the local population just as the Council of Magicians had. Everything reverted back to the old ways, even his use of slaves for life energy. It was, after all, the only way he could feed his dark power to grow it stronger.

Pilas, once a warm, tropical city, turned dark and cold after he gained power, shielded from the sun by a constant blanket of grey clouds. And the castle was no longer a beautiful harbinger of peace. It too was dank and dark, and that's the way he wanted it.

Druck sat on the stone slab throne and listened to slaves as they begged for his royal mercy. They were merchants, they said, from western Torm, a seaside village known for its shellfish and pearls. Their once elegant silk robes were dirty and ripped from months in the dungeon, and they were thin beyond recognition. They offered him riches beyond his imagination if he would just let them free.

He rather enjoyed hearing the pitiful pleas of prisoners. It fed his ego and confirmed his greatness and power. Of the thousands who had come before him, he hadn't let one go free, though, and these three were to be no exception. He waved his hand to the guards and told them to release the prisoner's chains. The three men bowed their heads and thanked him for his generous kindness. They vowed to return with a boat full of precious gems and jewels as soon as they could, and they turned to leave the room.

Druck smiled and brushed his black hair over his forehead. His eyes turned red and he spoke with a voice of a thousand souls, "Get back here you insolent fools. I'm not done with you!" The three men lifted off the ground and were spun around until they faced the magician. He raised his hand towards the levitating men. A white light swirled on their chest as their life energy was drained from their bodies. In a few seconds, beams of light shot from the swirling matter and was sucked into Druck's hand with a strong gust of wind. He closed his eyes, feeling the ecstasy of the new energy that filled his body. When he opened his eyes, he threw the three limp bodies to the floor with the flick of his finger, and ordered the guards to drag them to the ditch outside the city walls.

"My Lord!" called a middle-aged magician who just arrived. He stepped to the side to let the guards through the doorway and then proceeded to the throne. He lowered his head when he approached Druck and waited for a response.

"What is it, Grelius?" Druck asked, annoyed by his emissary's intrusion.

"I have news from Gornia that I believe you'll want to hear." The magician lowered his head once again in deference to Druck. He had followed the king since he had taken the throne and was awarded for his service by being given the opportunity to serve as chief negotiator between Druck and Leopold III of Gornia.

Druck sat up. "News from Gornia? What is it?"

"Leopold agreed. He's ready to sign the peace agreement. He will announce his decision in Tarsus in a few days." Grelius was happy to deliver the news. He'd worked hard to secure this agreement, and he was sure that he'd be rewarded with great wealth for his service.

Druck leaned forward and stared at his fair-skinned emissary. "I wanted the agreement a year ago," he said. "What has taken you so long? Were you enjoying the women of Tarsus too much to do my work?"

Grelius' heart sank when Druck spoke. His eyes grew large and his face filled with surprise. "M...My Lord," he stuttered. "I have worked ceaselessly since I arrived there. It took time to develop the relationships to make this happen. They were very skeptical of me for months. I...I..."

"Silence!" demanded Druck. "I told you to secure the agreement, and you failed to do it when I wanted it done! I have put other things in motion now that will settle the matter once and for all!"

Grelius stared at the floor while he was being reprimanded. This had not gone as he thought it would. "My Lord, may I inquire what the new plan is?" he asked.

"They have exhausted my patience! I will take them by force for their arrogance!" It had been his wish to wage war with them all along because he wanted revenge for the humiliating defeat of the council.

"My Lord, they are a powerful people. If we act rashly, we will…"

Druck stood up. "Rashly?! "Are you accusing me of something?!"

Grelius shook his head rapidly. "No, my Lord. I'm just being a cautious observer. I know what they're capable of."

"And do you know what I'm capable of?!"

"Yes, my Lord, I do."

"And yet you come to my throne and accuse me of acting irrationally? And you accuse me of being weak?!"

"No, my Lord. I didn't intend to imply any of that." Grelius stepped closer to the throne. "My Lord, we are at the precipice of peace. I advise that we take this opportunity and accept it."

Druck looked at his emissary with a scowl. He'd heard enough of this peace, and he was tiring of the ramblings of the useless advisor. He stood up and raised his hand, casting a ball of fire at the magician.

Grelius saw the attack in time. He placed a protective barrier around his body to deflect the incendiary magic and began to back out of the room towards the door he entered through.

Druck smiled and then sneered. His lip quivered with anger at the magician's audacity to defend himself. He threw his hand out in anger, and a massive fireball, three times the size of the first, floated in front of the throne. Druck pulled his arm back and whipped it forward sending the mammoth ball of fire at the magician. It exploded when it hit the barrier, and a shower of sparks floated to the ground in a cloud of smoke. When the smoke cleared, Grelius' burned remains were stuck to the floor in a smoldering heap.

"Does anyone else wish to question my judgment?!" shouted Druck. "Anyone?!" Everyone remained silent. "Let it be known…if you cross me, I will destroy you!" He looked around the room and saw everyone staring at the floor in deference to his power. He sat down, laughed, and leaned back against his thrown with a casual disregard for anyone who served him.

Chapter 18

Geoffrey went to bed as soon as he and Aidan returned from Lord Griswold's manor, but he couldn't sleep. Something was happening to Aidan, and he needed to know what it was. He remembered that Aidan complained about the old farmer who accused him of being a magician, and he knew it had something to do with what he saw earlier in the day. He just couldn't get that picture out of his mind. No matter how he tried to explain it, there was no way that his son could have done what he did without magic, and the magic he was thinking about had nothing to do with healing magic. Seeing his son standing over Tessera with his arms through her belly should have been an exhilarating moment. But it wasn't, and for obvious reasons. And his eyes were black as tar. Only magicians with the greatest power, he thought... master magicians of the highest order...could summon that kind of power. He didn't know. He'd never seen or heard of it before. Perhaps, he reckoned, Lord Nilet had something to do with it. He could have transferred his power to Aidan, he thought. But Aidan never had any contact with him. That couldn't be it. Only one possibility remained, and he wasn't ready to face it yet.

He finally fell to sleep three hours later, but it was a restless sleep full of the kind of vivid dreams one would have after drinking Billyroot tea. He tossed and turned for two more hours before falling into the deep sleep he needed.

Aidan knocked on the door and woke him up.

"Father, wake up. It's time to go," he said.

Geoffrey was so tired that he didn't remember dressing or getting on his horse. And he must have slept while on his horse because the next thing he knew, the four were arriving in Birkstow. He looked around and saw the three staring at him strangely. "What's the matter?" he asked.

"Glad you could join us," said Lord Barton. "We've been riding for eight hours, and you've been asleep the whole time."

That was strange. He'd never slept on his horse before, not even after being awake for two days at a time with a long ride ahead. "I...I'm sorry," he said. "It was a rough night."

Amelia pointed ahead at a small house at the edge of the village. "That's where he is," she said.

"Who?" asked Geoffrey. He didn't realize they were meeting someone in the sleepy village.

"Look," she said. "He's home."

Geoffrey saw a stream of smoke billowing out of the chimney. The house had a small wooden fence around it, and there were chickens and goats in the yard. A small chicken coop stood in the backyard next to a dead oak tree with thick, twisted branches rising to the sky. Something was hanging from a branch, but he couldn't make it out from where he was. He kept staring at it, and as they rode closer to the house, he could begin to make out the shape. Suddenly, he pulled hard on the reins of his horse and stopped. A look of terror filled his eyes.

Aidan stopped beside him. "What's wrong?"

Geoffrey pointed at the tree. "It's...it's...Annabel!"

Aidan looked at the body dangling from the limb

and laughed. "She didn't make it to Sherford, did she?"

Geoffrey was filled with rage, and his face turned bright red. "How dare you! She was part of our family, Aidan!" He stared long into his son's eyes and then spurred his horse to trot around the chicken coop until he was below her corpse. Vultures had eaten her eyeballs and had picked large chunks of skin out of her face, arms, and legs. He bent over in his saddle and vomited. "How could they?" he asked as he wiped his mouth with his sleeve.

Amelia rode beside him and stared at Annabel's body. "She was a good woman," she said. "But she was naïve. She never should have told us what she saw. She should have known."

Geoffrey turned towards her. "You mean, you did it?!" He couldn't believe what he was hearing.

"We had to protect ourselves," she said nonchalantly.

"She saw things she was never meant to see," said Lord Barton. "Now come on. We've got business here." The three of them rode to the house and dismounted from their horses and were tying them to a hitching post by the time Geoffrey approached. "You animals!" he shouted. "You're nothing more than animals!"

"Get off your horse and come in with us. Everything will make sense when you talk to him."

"Who is he?!" shouted Geoffrey. "Is he the person who did this to her?!"

"Yes," said Aidan calmly. "But after you talk to him, you'll understand everything." Aidan's eyes were glazed over as if he were in a trance.

Geoffrey hopped off his horse and grabbed his son's arm, spinning him around on the porch. "Aidan! Aidan!" Aidan stood and smiled, but he didn't say anything. He grabbed Geoffrey by the hand and led him into a dark, dirty room that smelled like rotting flesh. One window on the side of the room provided the only light. Geoffrey looked around. Animal bones hung from the rafters with twine, and skins were tacked all over the walls.

An old man was seated in a shadow in the far corner of the room. He wore a brown robe with a hood draped over his face, and he had a shepherd's crook in his left hand. He didn't move when the group walked in. Geoffrey nervously walked towards the man, noticing that his skin was grey with deep red spots scattered about. The last time he'd seen this was when he'd been called to check on a farmer. When he arrived, the old man was lying on the floor, dead for three weeks at least. That man's skin looked just like this. Geoffrey pulled the hood back. The old man's face was partially rotting away. His eyes had sunk into his skull, and the tip of his nose was missing. He was staring at the face when the old man's eyes opened wide and stared at him. Geoffrey fell backwards and landed on the floor hard.

"That's who we've come to see, father," said Aidan.

Amelia walked towards the old man and touched his shepherd's crook. "We are ready, my Lord," she said as she dropped to her knees and bowed her head.

Aidan stepped behind her. "If it is my destiny, my Lord, then I am willing." He dropped to his knees beside her and lowered his head.

Geoffrey tried to reach him, but Lord Barton held

him back. "Have you all gone mad?!" he yelled as he lurched forward against Lord Barton's grip. "Aidan! Listen to me son! Something's not right!"

The old man didn't seem to notice Geoffrey's pleas. His body cracked with the sound of breaking bones when he stood up, and he shuffled towards the two and stuck his hand over their heads. "Born of blood, living in flesh, empty in spirit," he said. His dried lips crumbled as he spoke. He slowly lowered his crook over their heads, reared back and struck Amelia in the head. Suddenly, his body seemed limber and strong, and he battered her skull with precise skill. She fell to the floor, blood running in streams down her head. Aidan didn't budge, and the old man turned to him. "Born of blood, living…"

"Aidan! Get up, Aidan," shouted Geoffrey. "You don't have to do this!" He fell to his knees and started to weep. "Aidan," he cried. "My son!"

For the first time, Aidan turned around and looked at his father. Geoffrey looked into his eyes. They were black, just like they were when he saved the baby. Aidan smiled and turned back to the old man obediently. "Born of blood, living in flesh, empty in spirit." And as he did to Amelia, he battered Aidan's head with the crook, crushing his skull with three blows.

Geoffrey lied on the ground and wept. Aidan was gone, and there was nothing he could do to help him. He grabbed hold of Lord Barton's legs and looked up with tearful eyes. "Why?! Why did you let this happen?! Why?! Why?!"

174

Geoffrey opened his eyes and jumped up. His heart was pounding in his chest, and he was breathing hard. "Aidan!" he yelled. "Aidan!" He heard a loud thump and then footsteps. His door flew open and Aidan ran into the bedroom.

"What's wrong?!" Aidan asked. "Did he return?" Aidan looked around the room, and when he was satisfied that no one was there, he sat at the foot of the bed. "Father," he said. "Are you alright?"

Geoffrey squinted through the darkness of the room and reached out to his son's face. He caressed his stubbly face and ran his fingers through his hair to make sure his skull was intact. "I...I just had a bad dream," he said.

"What was it about?" asked Aidan. He never knew his father to have nightmares.

Geoffrey lowered his legs to the floor. "I need some wine."

"The sun's almost up," said Aidan. "We leave in less than an hour."

Geoffrey shook his head and walked to the window. The sun was just beginning to rise over the Tasman hills east of the village. "I need..." he paused to think. "It can't be morning already."

"It is, and we need to get ready. We've got a long ride ahead of us."

Geoffrey turned to Aidan and reached his arm over his shoulders. "Have I ever told you how proud I am of you?" he asked.

"Yes you have, father. Many times."

Geoffrey's mouth opened as if he were ready to speak. There were things he needed to say, but he couldn't find the words. Aidan needed to know everything that was happening to him, he thought, but now was not the best time. Would there ever be a good time though? There were too many unanswered questions, and he hoped the journey in the Crokus' would provide the answers he needed. If he understood his dream correctly, Aidan's death wasn't real. It was symbolic. He wished he knew what it was symbolic of, however, but he had a suspicion that the key might lie near the beginning...the day when Aidan was born. Fate, after all, seemed to be revealing Aidan's destiny quite rapidly. He was of the right age, thought Geoffrey. He hugged Aidan instead, and the two watched the new sun rise slowly in the sky – just as his wife would have had it.

Chapter 19

Lord Barton couldn't sleep. It was the most difficult night he'd ever had. A week ago, life was
good. The weather had been pleasant, villagers joy-
fully prepared for their harvest, and peace prospered
throughout the region. But now, this idyllic place was
threatened with the prospect of war, and Heshire was
on the front line just as it was when his grandfather
lived. Worse than that, however, the Emperor knew
nothing about the threat of invasion as far as Lord
Barton knew. The army hadn't been dispatched, and
there was no guidance as to how to solve the problem
before it mushroomed out of his control. He only had
his instincts, and he wasn't even sure that they were
correct. The only things he knew for certain was that
Lord Nilet had been attacked by Druck, and three of
the Imperial Guard were killed with black magic. All
of the details, however, were left up to speculation.

He spent the night pouring over his father's journals hoping to discover how his grandfather would
have handled this situation. But there was nothing
there. Everything his father recorded about the early
days of the war indicated that the invasion came as
a total surprise, and his grandfather's actions were
nothing more than reactions to threats as they unfolded. And from the looks of things, they unfolded
at an alarming pace. Lord Barton found consolation in
one fact, however. At least he had time to seek out a
solution before the Sarcugians invaded. Perhaps fate
was working on his side in this respect, he thought. At
least he had a plan. And if he was successful in find-

ing this great healer magician then maybe he could stop the war before it began. But what if the man never existed? What if he had no bloodline? Those questions haunted Lord Barton throughout the night.

Out of desperation for an answer to any of the questions that bounced around his head, he went to his chamber and sat beside Lord Nilet who hadn't moved an inch since he'd been laid in the bed over two days ago. The old man's breath was shallow but regular. His skin was ashen grey. Lord Barton could tell that the master magician was withering away without food and water, and he knew that he had to find a way to remove Druck's spell before Lord Nilet died of starvation. But that was the least of everyone's problems. He needed to find out what Lord Nilet discovered while visiting Druck. He had to know what he knew so he could get the information to the Emperor. Gornia's fate rested upon Lord Nilet, and Lord Barton was frustrated that he could not remove the spell. It was his family's legacy – the power to heal magicians from spells. Centuries of knowledge woven into his cloak, and not one fiber of it contained the antidote to Druck's magic.

As Lord Barton listened to the old man breath, he decided to do what no young magician should do – read the master magician's mind. What choice did he have? If he could find something that could help, then he could be assured that his plan to cross into Sarcus was worthwhile. Perhaps he'd even be able to avoid doing so if he was able to see what Lord Nilet saw.

However, reading Lord Nilet's mind had its risks. Older magicians, especially master magicians of great power, often had defenses against intrusions such as this. His father had warned him about this while he was an apprentice. He told him stories about lesser magicians entering the consciousness of more power-ful men and being trapped in the greater magician's consciousness forever…a sentence of the soul only to be released once the physical body of either magi-cian withered and died. It was a dangerous prospect for Lord Barton, but he didn't know what else to do. He believed that Lord Nilet might still be aware on a subconscious level, and perhaps he would let him pass safely, especially considering the dire circumstances. Either way, Lord Barton had made up his mind to do it, and it was best to do it now when no one could con-vince him otherwise.

Lord Barton slid onto the bed's silk sheets and laid his hand on Lord Nilet's thigh. He took a deep breath and exhaled very slowly as he concentrated on the magic. After a few seconds, his eyes rolled back into his head and he went limp as his consciousness left his body. He hovered above the great magician for a few seconds as he contemplated the consequences once last time.

When used on mortals, Lord Barton could immedi-ately see what he wanted to see as soon as he entered their consciousness. It was like an open book, and all he had to do was flip through the pages of their lives until he found what he wanted. On magicians, how-ever, it was a different story. He'd only tried this on two magicians before. His father let him practice on him when he was an advanced apprentice. He also did it to Amelia before she started her apprenticeship. Neither opportunity turned out well.

His father's consciousness was protected with

advanced defenses, and all Lord Barton could remember about the experience was that he spent the entire time in total darkness, opening one door just to have another closed on him. His father eventually had to guide him out, and he never made any real progress at finding his father's true consciousness. Those were the longest and loneliest two hours he'd ever spent, and he remembered feeling as if he'd been locked in a small closet the whole time.

It was a totally different experience with Amelia. She didn't want her brother to come near her consciousness, but somehow her father convinced her to do so. Once he entered his younger sister's consciousness, he could see right into her life as if he'd been everywhere she'd been. At first, he saw drab things like playing outside with Aidan or riding her horse in the country. But after a while, he began to see things that he didn't like. He saw her filling his riding boots with horse manure, and he saw her snooping through his room and reading his diary. Furious, he exited her body and was ready to scold her. When he opened his eyes, his father and Amelia were laughing at him. When he started to tell his father what he saw, his father told him that those were planted memories, not real ones. After a few seconds, he chuckled at the joke as well, but he knew that the lesson had been an important one. Some traps are not dark and lonely. They can be misleading and cause you to make bad decisions. He remembered his father saying that these false memories can be placed in a magician by the magician himself or another magician.

As Lord Barton hovered in the dark bedroom, images of his father's warnings kept ringing in his ears.

He began to lower himself to Lord Nilet's face, but his father's warning got louder and louder. He stopped just short of entering the old man's nostrils. After a few seconds, he quickly moved back into his own body. By the time he opened his eyes, he knew that he'd made the right decision. Had he gone into Lord Nilet, he probably would have been trapped forever, or at least until the old man was released from Druck's spell.

He stood and covered Lord Nilet with the blanket. He'd have to rely upon his gut instincts after all, he thought.

Chapter 20

It was scalding hot by early afternoon, and they hadn't seen water since they'd crossed the Elbe hours ago. In fact, they hadn't seen any signs of life in the desert-like valley. The first mountain in the Crokus range hovered high above their heads as they followed an old road which was dotted with low-lying thorny shrubs and cactus. The arid land was dry, and it wasn't uncommon for the wind to blow sheets of dust at them as they trotted further into Sarcus toward their first destination, the small village of Birkstow.

"A little greenery would be nice about right now," Lord Barton said to Geoffrey as they trotted side-by-side. "I didn't expect it to be such a desert. Father's notes made it sound like a lush valley."

Geoffrey wiped the caked dirt from his lips and took a drink of water from his canteen. "Time has a way of changing the landscape," he said. "Perhaps this was their punishment for hiding the healer-magician."

"I just hope they didn't wipe out everyone else in the process," said Lord Barton.

Aidan looked at the first mountain in the range. There was something oddly familiar with this place. For some reason, he knew that Birkstow was on the other side of the mountain, hidden between two great peaks and fed by a fresh mountain stream. He could see the small, primitive huts lined on the banks of a stream, and visions of peasants doing their daily work flashed through his head. Those smiling faces of women and children were as real to him as the memories of his own childhood.

They were pleasant thoughts at first, but then it all turned ugly. Fire rained down upon the village from strange clouds. Charred corpses and homes smoldered throughout the valley. He saw an old woman's face. She was shaking, and tears streamed down her tough, wrinkled skin. It looked like she was holding something, but he couldn't make it out. He could only see part of her because the only sliver of sunlight came from a crack in the floorboards which she was hiding under.

Then he could smell the terrible odor of burnt flesh. He could hear the screams of people begging for a mercy that they would not get.

"Are you alright?" Amelia asked.

Aidan didn't hear her. His face twitched every time a new image popped into his head. The fear of that moment overcame him, and he started to weep for all of those people who died that day.

"Something's wrong with Aidan!" Amelia shouted.

Geoffrey swung his horse around, and Lord Barton followed. "Aidan!" shouted his father. He grabbed his son's reigns and pulled his horse close. He put a hand to Aidan's head. "He's hot. Has he had water lately?" he asked Amelia.

"Yes. Just a few minutes ago. We were talking, and then he went into this trance."

"Aidan!" said Lord Barton as he shook on his arm. "Wake up!"

Aidan looked at his father. "All those people are dead," he said.

"What do you mean?" asked Geoffrey as he rubbed his son's head. "Who is dead?"

"The villagers. I could see them."

"You could see them?" asked Lord Barton. "How?"

Aidan lifted his head. "I don't know. I just started seeing these people. I could see their village. It was so peaceful at first, and then it all changed. Fire from the sky, burned bodies, the smell of burned flesh. It was terrible."

Amelia put her hand underneath his cloak and rubbed his back. "It was just a bad dream," she said. "You must have fallen asleep."

Geoffrey shook his head. He didn't believe Aidan was dreaming. "Where was the village?" he asked.

Aidan pointed over the first mountain. It's on the other side. There's a large stream, and the village sat at the edge. It had one large street with homes and food stores sitting on both sides.

"Do you remember anything else?" asked Geoffrey.

"Just a bunch of faces. This one old woman in particular. It looked as if she were hiding from someone. She was protecting something. I'm almost sure it was a baby, but I'm not certain."

"What did she look like?" asked Amelia.

"She had a weathered face," said Aidan. Her eyes were blue, and her hair black, but it was peppered with a lot of grey. She looked so kind."

"What happened to her?" asked Lord Barton.

"I don't know. Everything turned black, and then I woke up."

Geoffrey bit his lip and didn't say anything else. He patted his son on the neck and handed him some water. When Aidan finished drinking, he turned his horse towards the mountain and started a slow gallop up the winding road.

"Why's he in such a hurry?" asked Amelia.

Lord Barton stared at his trusted healer as he rode away. "I don't know. Something's bothering him. We'd better move before he gets away from us." He looked at Aidan. "Are you alright now?"

"Yes. I'm fine. I'm ready to ride."

Amelia patted his back. "It was just a bad dream, OK?" she consoled. "Everyone has them every now and then." She leaned over and kissed him softly on the lips. "I love you," she whispered. "Don't you ever forget that."

Aidan smiled. He needed to hear that.

"Now let's go before those two lose us for good. I'd hate to get lost out here."

Aidan smiled and spurred his horse forward. Somehow, though, he knew he wouldn't get lost. He knew this place better than anyone else. He just didn't know how.

Geoffrey reached the top of the mountain before anyone else, and what he saw amazed him. They'd been travelling in a desert all day, and the side of the mountain they climbed was nothing but rock and dirt, bare as bare can be. It was a different world on the other side. And, as far as he could see, it was green. He reached around, pulled out his canteen, and uncorked it with his teeth. He took several gulps of water when he heard the first birds singing. This place was full of life, he thought, but how could that be?

Lord Barton trotted up a minute later. He looked over at the valley below. "Impossible," he said. He reached for his canteen as well.

"Impossible but nonetheless real," said Geoffrey. "I don't understand it either." He tied his canteen back to his saddle and turned to look for Aidan and Amelia. "Could it be magic?"

Lord Barton shook his head as he swallowed a mouthful of lukewarm water. "Nothing like I've ever seen," he said. "The power it would take to do this. It's impossible."

"Even for Druck?"

"No black magic did this," said Lord Barton. "If this is magic, then it brought life, not death. I know of no magician who could do this."

Amelia and Aidan finally caught up with the group. Aidan looked out over the valley. "This is where it started," he said.

"What started?" asked Amelia.

"The beginning."

"What do you mean by that?" asked Lord Barton. He jumped off his horse and walked towards Aidan.

"I don't know," said Aidan. He dismounted and walked to the edge of the road and looked down. He pointed down below. "See that stream?"

They looked down the side of the mountain to the very bottom of the valley. A large stream snaked along the edge of the mountain.

"That's where the village was."

"Birkstow?" asked his father.

"I guess. It was destroyed by fire that came from the sky."

Lord Barton leaned against a tree. He rubbed his

chin. "Now that sounds like black magic to me."

"I don't know what it was," said Aidan. "It was frightening, and all the people were killed except this old woman."

Amelia walked towards Aidan and put her arm around him. "It was just a dream," she said. "I'm sure we'll find that the village is still there."

Aidan smiled. "You're probably right. This whole trip has spooked me for some reason. I guess my mind's a little over-active right now."

Geoffrey knew there was more to Aidan's dream than a dream. He just didn't know how or why Aidan knew the things that he knew. Aidan was right, though. This was where it all started, at least for him.

"We should get down there before nightfall," said Lord Barton. Our horses need the rest and a long, cool drink."

Geoffrey leaned against his horse before mounting and took a deep breath. He had to tell Aidan the truth soon. He dreaded it, but uncovering all the mystery had to begin soon, and there was no better place to tell him than Birkstow.

Chapter 21

Lord Griswold didn't speak to Lord Bline during their ride to Heshire. He was incensed at the humiliation he underwent the day before, and he was afraid. The past two days rattled his nerves, and he felt like he was losing his sanity. His father's visit the night before was enough to shake him. Then last night…well, he'd rather not think about last night. Hanging high above this, though, was the worst of it all. He was being asked to use these new powers against his friend. He knew what his father told him, and he knew that Lord Bline had confirmed it, yet he still didn't want to believe it. Barton and Amelia were good magicians and benevolent rulers. They were everything that he wasn't, yet was he to believe they were really conspiring against the Emperor to bring Gornia down to its knees? It didn't make sense. But, what choice did he have? He accepted his father's amulet, and he was overpowered by Bline's superior magic. He felt helpless to do anything, and that made him angrier and angrier as he rode behind the powerful magician.

And why him, he thought? Why couldn't Bline stop Barton by himself? He was certainly powerful enough to do it. Why did they need him to do it? These questions haunted him, and the more he thought about it, the more he began to believe that this was some sort of conspiracy. Perhaps he'd even been caught in one of Druck's traps.

Bline brought his horse to a halt and waited for Griswold to catch up. "You're having second thoughts again, aren't you?" he said with his pretentious accent.

He flicked his long hair over his shoulder as he turned to face the wary magician.

"How do you know what I'm thinking?" Griswold replied. He was beginning to hate the arrogant Bline with each passing moment.

"I sense it, good fellow. Now pray tell me…you aren't still upset about our little fun last night are you?" He smirked and acted like it was all a bunch of nothing.

Griswold grabbed his amulet tightly. He thought about trying to see how powerful his new magic was. He wanted to incinerate this pompous fool here and now. "Let me ask you something, Lord Bline. If you're so powerful and important, why can't you track down Barton and handle the situation by yourself?"

Bline smiled. He could tell the young magician wanted to use his amulet, and he was more than happy to let him try. "You are a petty, petty little magician, aren't you? Look at you. You think that daddy's little amulet is going to settle a score, don't you?" He flicked his hand up into the air. "Well, go ahead little man…try it. See what it gets you? Humor me."

Griswold thought hard. He fingered the emerald nervously as he stared into Bline's eyes.

"You're angry with me," laughed Lord Bline. "Oh so angry. Be a good boy and do something about it. You might get your answer if you do…or you might die. Either way would be a good outcome as far as I'm concerned. I have other things I could be doing right now."

As soon as Bline said 'die,' Griswold let go of the amulet and sank deep into the saddle. He wasn't prepared to test his new power on him. He had no idea what he could do, and he surely wasn't ready to find out. "Just answer the question," he mumbled.

Bline laughed. "I knew you didn't have it in you. You're as much of a coward as I suspected. But a good choice, I have to agree. A good choice for you today."

"Can you just tell me the answer because I don't understand why I am needed."

Bline sat high in his saddle. His faced creased with anger. "Oh, the little boy demands answers! Does he wish to manage vineyards or become great?! Which is it? Wine or country, boy?!" Bline's voice was deep and coarse, and it sent shivers down Griswold's spine.

"I...I..."

"I WHAT?!" demanded Bline. His face turned red with anger.

"I guess I want to do what's best for Gornia," mumbled Griswold. He stared at the ground like a child being reprimanded by his father. "I'd just like to know why I'm here."

Bline was not about to tell Griswold anything that would make him think. He needed him to follow, to be obedient, and, above all, to be loyal. It was for his good as well. Griswold would not like the truth. It would be best if he learned the truth when he had no other choice than to accept it.

Griswold finally gathered the courage to look Bline in the eye. "Well?"

"Well, the truth is that I cannot fight the combined power of Druck, Nilet, and Barton at the same time. Your father reached out to from the spirit world and said that he would assist me with this great task. You are the one he chose to carry out his part."

Griswold shook his head slowly. "What does my

father care about Gornia? He's dead!"

Bline pulled his stallion beside Griswold and gently cupped the amulet in his gloved hand. "When we die, we go to a higher consciousness...magicians that is. We do not lose our love of family or country in the afterlife. In fact, it becomes more a part of us than ever, just on a higher plane. Your father was a great magician...greater than you'll ever know. His power will be the key to our victory." He released the amulet. As it dropped against Griswold's chest, Bline patted him on the shoulder. "It's a pity you didn't get to know your father. He was a great magician."

Griswold stared at the amulet. "Did you know him?"

Bline laughed. "We had our share of good times," he said. He pulled his horse around. "Come on. I'll tell you more on the way to Heshire." And he rode away.

The two magicians rode through the night. It was sunrise when they arrived at Heshire. Contrary to what Bline told him the day before, he spoke nothing of his father. He had told the truth, he reasoned, but not the whole truth. That was for another day. He just told the young magician what he needed to hear to keep him from doing something stupid. It was more important to keep him in the plan

They pulled their exhausted mounts to a halt as soon as they could see the village gates. "What do we do now?" asked Griswold. He was tired and wanted to rest, and they needed new horses as well.

Bline, however, looked as fresh as he did when they left Werth. Griswold couldn't understand how he fared so well on such a harsh journey, nor could he wrap his head around how he looked so young. He knew that Bline had to be much older. He said he knew his father for one thing, and he also had great power, and that power only comes with age.

"We change here," said Bline. He dismounted, closed his eyes, and waved a hand in front of his face. By the time Griswold blinked, Bline had completely changed his looks. He now looked like a lowly peasant. His hair was scraggly, his teeth were bad, and his clothes were typical of a peasant – filthy, ragged, and worn. Bline looked at Griswold and smiled. "Your turn now." Even his voice had changed.

"Ah...I don't know how to change my appearance," said Griswold. He scratched his sweat-soaked head as he tried to come up with a spell.

"Sure you can," said Bline. "It's as easy as making yourself invisible."

Griswold chuckled. "Yes, well I can't do that either."

Bline shook his head. "You couldn't do it last week, but I bet you can now. Just think it, and it will be with a wave of your hand."

Griswold stared blankly at Bline.

"Your amulet, stupid!" Bline shouted. "You have powers that you never had before. Use them or so help me, I'll turn you into a damn dog!"

Griswold climbed off his horse and held the amulet in his hand. He closed his eyes, thought the thought and waved his hand. When he opened his eyes, he could see that Bline was pleased.

"Well done! Well done indeed."

Griswold looked at his arms. They were dirty. His clothes were filthy, and he stank. Even his boots had holes in them. He couldn't believe that he'd done it. "And our horses?" he asked.

Bline raised his hand and both horses disappeared. "We'll get new ones in Heshire," he said.

"What's our plan?" asked Griswold. He knew that Barton had left the village, and the only person left of importance was Nilet. "Are we to take Nilet?"

"No. We just rest, eat, and drink. Perhaps we can learn something about their departure from the locals."

"What about Nilet?" asked Griswold. "Shouldn't we get him?"

"You mean kill him?" asked Bline. "No. We need to find out what he knows first, and we won't be able to get that information until later. His time will come, though."

"Then what are we doing here?" asked Griswold.

"We rest. We will need all of our energy for tomorrow." He turned and looked at Griswold. "And we gather as much information as we can about where they went when they left town."

Griswold was confused. "Why can't we track them with magic?"

"And risk their detecting us before we get there? Give them a chance to ambush us? No way. We track them like mortals, and we surprise them!"

"I still don't understand how Barton and his sister are such a threat. He is no more powerful than I am... uh, was."

"Ah, but he has a strong ally. Someone possibly

stronger than you or I put together."

"Druck?"

Bline started walking towards Heshire. "Something like that. Now let's go."

Chapter 22

The sun had already dropped below the mountains by the time the four reached the lush valley. It was a long, treacherous descent. It was obvious the road hadn't been used in years because it was overgrown and was littered with fallen tree limbs. At one point, they had to dismount and lead their horses over a small oak that had fallen over the road. One thing was sure, however. There was no sign of human life down there. But the calming sound of flowing water made it a good place to camp for the night nonetheless.

"I'm certain this is where the village was," said Aidan as he dismounted. He knew that no one believed him, but he also knew that he hadn't lost his mind. He didn't remember it being so overgrown, but everything around him felt familiar.

"When the sun rises, we'll get a better look at this place," said Lord Barton. "There's no need to worry about it now."

They unsaddled their horses and led them to the spring before they started to make camp. Lord Barton lit a fire in a clearing, and Amelia laid blankets out for everyone. The spring made the air feel damp, and as the sun set, the air turned cool. The fire felt good, even after riding in sweltering heat through a desert all day.

"I just can't believe how different it is on this side of the mountain," said Amelia. "It doesn't feel right." An owl called out in the dark just as she spoke as if it were an omen confirming everything she felt.

"We can't worry ourselves with thoughts like that right now," said Lord Barton. "We need to rest first. We can find out where we are in the morning." He pulled close to the fire and pulled out his map. Sure enough, they were on the correct road, and this was where Birkstow was marked. He looked at Aidan as he ate a piece of chicken that Amelia had warmed for him. How could he have known so much? Was it just a hallucination brought on by the heat, or was something else going on?

Amelia handed Geoffrey a warmed chicken breast. She could tell that something heavy was bothering him. "He's going to be alright," she told him. "I'll keep an eye on him tomorrow."

Geoffrey smiled. She had no idea what tomorrow was going to bring for Aidan. He didn't either. He knew he'd have to talk to his son about some things in the morning, and he was scared that Aidan would not take it well. But he had to have that talk. It was time to piece some things together. He knew Aidan's vision and his memory of this place had to have something to do with what he did when he delivered Tessera's baby. After witnessing that, nothing seemed strange to him anymore. He knew it was all connected, and it began right here many years ago. That, he was certain.

"Thank you, Amelia," said Geoffrey. "I know you will."

She put her hand on his and rubbed it. "He'll be alright."

The sun just started to rise when they woke.

Unbeknownst to them, they had camped right in the middle of an old village square. An abandoned well was no more than fifty paces from their campfire. The wooden platform had rotted, leaving a rusted iron frame hanging above a large hole.

Aidan was the first to look around. It was overgrown, but he could remember where the villager's homes were. He quickly walked west and started looking for anything that resembled a shelter. He found pots and dishes partially covered in moss and dirt, and then he found rusted tools at another location. He turned and ran towards the other side of the campsite. Everyone just stared as he searched.

"Here it is!" he yelled.

Geoffrey ran over to him. "What is it? What have you found?"

"This is where the old woman hid." He pointed to a hole in the ground near the stream.

"What old woman?" asked Lord Barton.

"The old woman who I saw in my vision! It was real. It was just as if I was there."

Amelia turned to her brother. "Has a spell been cast upon him?" She had hoped that the night's rest would have made things better, but it hadn't.

"I sense nothing," whispered her brother. He looked around and scanned the sky. "But there is something about this place that defies explanation. I can't tell if it's magic or not. If it is, then it's more powerful than you or I have ever seen."

"That anyone's ever seen," replied Amelia. She pulled her hair into a ponytail and tied it with a piece of lace. "Something's affecting him, and it scares me. I wish we could just go back to Heshire."

"Perhaps that's the point. If this is some sort of black magic, then maybe the point is to drive us out."

Aidan stood at the pit and stared. It was so real. He'd never felt this way before, and trying to explain it was impossible. These deep-seated feelings were too much for him to understand, let alone anyone else. He staggered away and walked towards the muddy bank of the stream where he could be alone in his thoughts.

Geoffrey motioned towards Amelia and Lord Barton. "May I have a few minutes alone with him?" he whispered.

Lord Barton nodded his head. "Please do." He pointed up the stream. "We'll go up there and try to find a road that leads us out of here. Perhaps there's a village nearby."

"Thank you. I think it will help." Geoffrey turned around and walked towards Aidan.

"Geoffrey," cried Amelia.

Geoffrey turned around. "Yes?"

"If he needs me, I'll be right back. Will you let him know that?"

Geoffrey nodded. "I'm sure he'll need you. Don't you worry."

Geoffrey found Aidan downstream. He was sitting on a log and had his feet hanging in the cool water. A tall oak towered over the water and provided nice shade from the early morning sun. Aidan watched a bullfrog jump from stone to stone as it made its way to the other side.

"I see you found a nice spot," said Geoffrey as he

approached. "Great place to relax."

Aidan smiled. "I don't understand why everything seems so familiar." He pointed to a large boulder in the middle of the stream. "Like that rock. The
kids who lived here used to fish from there." Then he
pointed to the left of the rock. "And right there. I bet
it gets a lot deeper right there. It used to be a good
swimming hole." He lifted his feet out of the water.
"And this is where they'd cool the milk. They only had
two cows."

Geoffrey shook his head. The fact that he remembered so much amazed him. "Aidan," he said calmly.

"Yes, father."

He put his hand on Aidan's shoulder. "I need to
talk to you about something."

Aidan turned and looked at him. He seemed
older than usual and tired. He stood and grabbed
his father's shoulders. "Hey. Don't you worry. I'll be
alright."

Geoffrey smiled. "I know you will, son. I'm not
worried about it. I think I can help explain some of it
to you though."

"What's the matter?" asked Aidan. He slid over
and pointed to the log. "Let's sit and talk."

Geoffrey wiped a tear from his eye. He hadn't
cried since his wife died, but he felt like another part
of him was getting ready to die. This was the moment he'd dreaded for years. "You're mother loved
you so much," he muttered as he fought back more
tears. "And you know that I do as well. We've always
been…" He couldn't finish.

Aidan rubbed his father's back. It was difficult to
see him hurt so much.

"We've always been so proud of you."

"I know you have. And I couldn't have been luckier to have had great parents like you. I wouldn't be who I am today were it not for you."

Geoffrey looked at Aidan . "Your mother would kill me for telling you what I am about to tell you, but I don't know any way around it anymore."

Aidan leaned back. What was his father getting ready to tell him? His stomach felt like it was going to come right out of his mouth. "Tell me what?" he asked.

"Your mother and I tried to have children for years with no success. I knew she couldn't conceive long before she did. I just didn't have the heart to tell her that she was sterile."

"What do you mean by 'sterile?'" asked Aidan. He didn't like where this was going.

Geoffrey stood and walked into the stream a few steps. He kept his back turned to Aidan. "When she was a child, she had a bad case of fever that went un-treated for too long. It sterilized her."

"How was...?"

Geoffrey balled his fist. "Just let me finish!" he shouted. He turned and looked at Aidan. He could tell that he was scaring him. "I'm so sorry," he said. "I have something that I need to say, and it's very diffi-cult for me."

Aidan nodded. "It's alright. I won't interrupt you again." Inside, he was tied in knots. He wasn't sure that he wanted to hear anymore.

"Like I said, I didn't have the heart to tell your mother. But as we got older, she became more desper-ate than ever to get pregnant. She knew that she was running out of time." He paced back and forth. This was more difficult than he thought. "I had to tell her," he said, "and it hurt like hell to let her know."

Aidan leaned forward and picked up a stick and started drawing circles in the mud. He couldn't look at his father, so he kept his eyes focused on the ground.

"She hated me at first," Geoffrey said. "She didn't leave the house for days. But over time, she realized that I had been trying to protect her." Geoffrey turned around. "And that's when we decided to look for you." He paused and stared at Aidan. He wanted to see some kind of reaction, but he got nothing other than a glancing look.

Geoffrey sat on the log. "You came to us when we needed you the most," he said. "I was called to a shepherd's house not far from where we crossed the Elbe yesterday. While I was there, we heard a woman yelling for help. We ran outside and saw her standing on the other side of the river. She begged us to come to her, but when we hesitated, she started to cross by herself. And she was holding a bundle in her arms. When she got to deeper water, she held the bundle on top of her head. We were so shocked that we couldn't move. We'd never seen anyone from the other side, and we didn't know what to do. The woman made it across, but she collapsed on the riverbank. I ran to her only to find that the bundle she was carrying was a little baby."

Aidan looked at his father. "That baby was me, wasn't it?"

Geoffrey could hear the hurt in his voice, and it made it very difficult to finish. He cleared his throat and tried to talk but nothing came out.

Aidan grabbed his father's hand and held it tightly. "It's alright. You can tell me."

"Yes," mumbled Geoffrey. It felt so good to let it out. He took a deep breath and sighed. "It was you."

"What happened to the old woman? Was she the one I saw in my vision?"

"You described her perfectly. I don't know how you remember. You were no more than six months old when she brought you to me."

"Did she tell you anything?"

Geoffrey took another deep breath. "I tried to help her, but she was so old and had walked a long way. She was dehydrated and had terrible blisters on her feet. I don't think she'd eaten for days. She died that night. I think she held off the inevitable until she found someone to leave you with."

"But did she tell you anything about me?"

Geoffrey stood and folded his arms. "She was delirious. She said a lot of things. Most of it was gibberish."

Aidan stood and faced his father. "Well, it had to have meant something. What did she tell you?"

Geoffrey walked away from Aidan and kept his back turned to him. "She said that you were a special child. She said some men killed everyone in her village because they were looking for you." Geoffrey bit his lip before finishing. "She said you would one day change the world as we knew it."

Aidan shook his head. "Why would you hide this from me all these years?"

"Because!" shouted Geoffrey. "I thought the old woman was out of her mind. And your mother and I did not want you to think that we were not your parents! We made a pact with each other that we would never tell you any of this."

Aidan grabbed his father's shoulder to force him to look into his eyes. "Is that why you never wanted to teach me the magic of healing? I wasn't born of your blood, so I'd never possess it?"

Geoffrey looked at the ground. "Yes."

"So why did you teach me to become a healer then? Was this some sort of game to you?"

Geoffrey grabbed his son's arm. "Never! I thought I could teach you to be a fine healer. You didn't have to have the magic to heal everyone. I taught you everything I knew, and you've become a fine healer. I'm proud of you."

Aidan unclasped his cape and dropped it on the ground. "I guess I don't need this anymore," he said. "Thanks for the lie." He started to walk away as tears welled in his eyes. "I guess Amelia and I can never marry now," he said. He walked towards the woods.

Geoffrey grabbed the cape and followed him. "Aidan! Wait!" He grabbed him by the arm and swung him around. "I'm not finished!" He handed him the cape. "Just let me finish."

Aidan couldn't look his father in the eyes, so he stared across the stream while he talked.

"Do you remember how you saved that little baby the other day?"

"No. I think I passed out and you came in and saved the day. How could I have done anything? I'm not your blood, remember?"

"Stop it!" Geoffrey's eyes lit up and he put both hands on his boy's shoulders. "Look at me, please."

Aidan lowered his eyes and looked at his father.

"You did something amazing. I've never seen anything like it in my entire life. When I came back with the water, I saw you standing over Tessera with both arms in her stomach. You pulled the baby out without hurting her. I saw it with my own eyes!" He started to laugh. "The old lady wasn't going senile after all!"

Aidan felt lightheaded. He bent over and sat on the ground. "I had my arms in her stomach? And I pulled the baby out?"

"Yes!"

"Why didn't you tell me that either?"

"Because I needed time to figure it out for myself. I had to find something that could explain it, but there was nothing. That's why I locked myself in the library all afternoon when we got home. I was searching for an answer, and the answer was always there. That old woman was protecting something more valuable than just another child, and she knew it."

Aidan started to tremble. "What am I?"

Geoffrey hugged him. "You're my son, and I love you very much. I don't know whose child you were, nor do I understand anything, but I have a strong feeling that we're going to find out something real soon." He helped Aidan to his feet. "I know you don't believe in fate, but I do, and I know that your fate will be revealed on this side of the river."

Aidan took the cape and clasped it around his neck. "Have you told Lord Barton or Amelia any of this?"

"No. It wouldn't have been right."

"Should I?"

Geoffrey cupped Aidan's face in his hands. "I'm so

sorry that I had to tell you this, but you need to know. Too many things have happened to you over the past few weeks, and if I didn't tell you, I'm afraid that you would have gone crazy trying to figure everything out for yourself."

Aidan's head was spinning. He had a lot on his mind and had so many questions. Too much was happening too fast. "I need some time alone," he said.

"Are you sure you're alright?" asked his father.

Aidan shook his head. "I don't know what I'm feeling right now. I'm just numb." He walked towards the woods. "I just need some time, that's all."

Geoffrey watched Aidan until he was no longer in sight. He dropped to his knees and looked up. "I'm so sorry I had to tell him, honey," he mumbled. "I'm so sorry."

Chapter 23

"Wake up!"

Griswold rolled over, rubbed his eyes, and yawned. He'd had a terrible night and didn't fall to sleep until early in the morning. He'd never slept on hay before, and he vowed never to do so again.

"I said get up!"

"Wha...wha...what!" He sat up and swung his fist into the air, almost striking Bline in the face.

"You fool! You almost hit me!"

Griswold pushed back against the haystack. "I... I'm sorry," he said. "You frightened me. I almost forgot that we changed our appearance yesterday."

"I'll change yours permanently if you don't get up. We've got to go. It's starting."

Griswold stood and stretched. "What's starting?"

"Barton is where he shouldn't be. We need to make haste and find him."

Griswold brushed the hay off his sleeves and pants. "It's a good thing that drunk guard told us where Barton crossed the river," said Griswold.

Bline looked out the stable door towards the distant mountains. Yes it is, and I know exactly where he is. Now let's get moving!"

Griswold grabbed Bline's sleeve. "Hold on for a second. Why don't we get some food first and then transport ourselves there? Why do we need to go through the trouble of travelling?"

Bline snickered. "Do you know how difficult that it is? You fool! Just because you have some new powers does not mean you're ready to use them. Transportation spells take a lot of energy, and even the most powerful magicians have to rest for days after such a trick." Bline walked outside. "We'll need to be ready when we face Barton. We can't risk such a move."

Griswold never thought about it before. After all, he never really had much power until now. But he could imagine how great it would be to be all-powerful and never have to worry about draining oneself. He chuckled. That must be the stuff of legend.

Geoffrey sat alone at the edge of the stream for over an hour before Lord Barton and Amelia returned. He was a mess right now, and he could only imagine what Aidan was going through. Perhaps it wasn't a good idea to tell him, he thought. But then again, Aidan would eventually find out for himself if these odd things kept happening to him. Geoffrey didn't know what was right anymore, and he prayed that he did the best thing for his son.

Amelia was winded by the time she reached Geoffrey. She and her brother had hiked up the road leading out with the hopes of finding another village nearby. They crested a large hill nestled between the two mountains, but they didn't see anything that resembled a village in the distance, so they came back to get the horses so they could go.

"We've got to mount up," she said as she caught her breath. "There's nothing around here." She took a deep breath and looked around. "Where's Aidan?"

"Taking a walk in the woods. He needs to be alone for a while."

Lord Barton leaned against a tree while taking a drink from his canteen. "We need to get over that mountain by dusk. I thought I smelled smoke when we were out, so I'm hoping the first village is on the other side."

Geoffrey threw a pebble into the stream and watched it skip twice before sinking into the water. "He needs time right now. Perhaps we should camp here another night before we head out."

Amelia stepped towards Geoffrey and put her hand on his back. "Geoffrey, what's going on with him? Is there something that I need to know? I mean, two days ago, he was fine, but since we've come here, it's as if he's a different person. I've never seen him like this before, and it frightens me."

Geoffrey turned around and placed his hand on top of hers. "Perhaps it would be best if he told you in his own time."

Lord Barton was less patient than his sister. He pushed off the tree and corked his canteen. "I understand that he's not feeling well, but we cannot forget what we came here to do. We have to find a solution for Lord Nilet. We don't have time on our side, and we certainly can't wait here until he's ready to come out of the woods."

Geoffrey stood and faced the young magician. He felt older than ever right now, and he wasn't sure that he was up to the task of moving on quite yet. "He is dealing with some things that even I don't understand. And he's also coping with the fact that some things haven't been the way he thought they were. That's all I can say right now. The rest will have to come from him. I don't know where he went, and I don't want to drag him out until he's ready."

"Do you suggest that we let fate decide the future of Gornia while we wait?" asked Lord Barton. He was becoming impatient, and his voice clearly showed his frustration.

Amelia stepped between the two men. "Hold on, brother. Perhaps it wouldn't hurt to camp here one more night. If fate is to determine our destiny, then who's to say that fate won't lead us to our answer here?"

Lord Barton shook his head. "Our fate is in our own hands right now. We agreed that we'd come here to look for answers. I never said anything about waiting for them to come to us."

Geoffrey turned to face Lord Burton. "I am sorry that this has become an issue. I truly am. But if Aidan and I are to be of service to you, then we must wait for him. Perhaps you and Amelia should go ahead without us. We could catch up to you tomorrow or the next day."

Amelia looked at her brother and shook her head. "That's not a viable option, and you know it. We need to stick together."

Lord Barton considered Geoffrey's offer. It did make sense, he reasoned. He looked at his sister and said, "I think that's what we should do."

Amelia's face wrinkled with anger. "That's not right! I am not leaving them here all alone! If you want to go ahead, then by all means, go. You're certainly capable of handling yourself! I'm staying with them!"

Lord Barton stomped his foot on the ground. "We don't have time to kill, little sister! We've got to find an answer, and we've got to find it soon!" He pointed towards Heshire. "Lord Nilet is all that stands between Druck and Gornia, and I'm going to do everything I can to stop him before thousands are killed! If you want to stay here and take care of your love, then do it! But I hope it doesn't come at the cost of a life!" By the time he finished yelling, he knew he'd crossed the line. He turned around and kicked the tree he'd been leaning against and walked a few paces towards the stream. He was frustrated, and he was upset that he had spoken so harshly. He hoped they knew he didn't mean what he said.

Amelia picked up a small rock and threw it towards her brother. It hit the ground at his feet. "You're such an ass sometimes," she said. "They've served Heshire well, and this is how you treat them?" She walked towards him. "And how dare you use my love for Aidan against me! There is no way that our relationship could be responsible for one death!"

Geoffrey had heard enough. He stood up and walked between the two. "Let's calm down a little."

Lord Barton backed up and looked at both of them. "I'm sorry," he said. "I didn't mean anything I said. It was inappropriate."

"But your motives are not," said Geoffrey. "You have a great burden on your shoulders, and your mission is our mission."

"Geoffrey's right. We should stick together," replied Amelia. Her voice still contained a hint of hostility towards her brother.

"Now, now…I didn't say that," said Geoffrey. "If Lord Barton feels that he must move on, then he must. And if he does, Amelia, I think you should go with him. None of us should be alone. We know nothing of this place, and there could be dangers around every bend."

Lord Barton took a deep breath. "We will wait," he said. "We need to go together."

Amelia smiled, relieved that they were not going to leave Geoffrey and Aidan by themselves. She also felt happy that she'd be able to talk to Aidan at length when he returned so that she could help him through his crisis…whatever it may be.

Chapter 24

Aidan's head was spinning in circles. In just a few minutes, his father had turned his entire life upside down, and he needed to get away from everyone, especially him. The deeper he walked into the woods, the sicker he felt. He just wanted to catch his breath, but every time he tried, it felt like someone sucked the air right back out of his lungs. He couldn't even concentrate enough to watch his step across the uneven forest floor. He bounced from tree to tree, tripping on small stones, holes, and fallen branches.

He didn't know where he was going, and he didn't care. It didn't even matter if he got lost. Nothing mattered anymore. He was lost in a much bigger way, and life didn't matter to him. All that he knew was a façade – a forgery designed by him mom and dad designed to give him a false life. Now that he knew the truth, he had become nothing more than a hollow shell of what he used to be. A forgotten soul trapped between the real world and the Netherlands.

Then, there was this mumbo-jumbo about his having some kind of mystical power. He laughed when he recalled his father's story. Supposedly, he'd saved that baby's life by sticking his arms through Tessera's stomach and pulling him out using some unknown form of magic. What sort of fool does he think I am, he thought? Was he trying to make me feel better? Did he think that would make up for the lies he'd been told all his life?

Aidan staggered to a large oak tree and plopped down. He grabbed his head and squeezed as hard as he could. "Stop spinning!" he yelled. "Please!" He grabbed a small branch off the ground and threw it. "Why me?!" His voice bounced off the trees, but no one answered.

And if that were not enough, he had just found love. Amelia would certainly not have him as a husband now. It was a big step for her to marry a healer instead of another magician, but when she finds out that he's not even a true healer, she'll have no choice but to marry someone else. Magicians are forbidden to marry mortals, so there was no escape from this life sentence. Sure, she would tell him that it's alright right now, but when she returns to her uncle's home, time and distance will make it easier for her to slowly and painfully break it off with him. He might as well come to terms with that right away. It would just be easier if he were to push her away first.

Everything made him angry. He slammed his fist into the ground and staggered to his feet. "I'll never forgive you!" he shouted, hoping that Geoffrey could hear him. He wished he had not gone so easy on him when they talked. He wished that he had screamed and shouted at the old man. But he didn't, and that made him angrier. Fighting back tears, he ran as hard as he could towards the stream. He just wanted to get away – far away from anyone who knew him – far away from his former life.

He must have been further from the stream than he thought because it felt like he'd been running for hours. Out of breath and weak, he slid onto his knees and slumped over in exhaustion. This would be just as good of a place to die as any other, he thought as he sucked air.

"Would you believe that the entire world was created right where you are kneeling?"

Aidan lurched around so fast that he fell on his bottom. He could swear that he heard someone talking to him, but he didn't see anyone. His heart pounded in his ears. Perhaps this was another hallucination, he thought.

"My brother and I created your world out of nothing. We had so many plans for your kind."

The voice sounded like it came from behind him. He quickly clamored to his feet and turned around. Again, no one was there.

"It became a grand experiment, really, to see how humans could treat each other without our intervention."

Aidan swung around once again. If this was a hallucination, then it was a good one. Once more, there was no one near him.

"But we learned that man needed more than just a simple existence, so we showed ourselves, and they worshipped us. It was good to be loved, and we repaid them by giving the gift of magic and healing to those who loved us most, and we promised to allow those gifts to be passed to their children and their children's children."

Aidan whirled around again. "Show yourself!" he screamed.

"But then man did what man has always done. He chose to love either me or my brother, and that is where your history begins."

"Who are you?!" cried Aidan. He felt a hand touch his shoulder. He spun around so fast that he fell down once again. Standing above him was an old man with a long white beard dressed in a white robe. Aidan slid backwards on the ground to try to get away.

The old man held his arms out wide. "No harm will come to you." He voice sounded as if he spoke with a thousand voices, and his aura glowed like the sun. "I mean you no harm."

"Who...who are you?" His lips quivered and a cold chill went down his spine. Fear and panic swept through his body.

"I am you, and you are me," replied the man.

For the first time, Aidan saw the man's eyes. They were as black as lumps of coal. "Wha...what kind of answer is that?" asked Aidan.

"The correct one, I must admit," said the old man. He smiled and motioned for Aidan to come closer. "Come to me child," he said. "I won't harm you."

Aidan felt sick with fear. He wanted to run, but he couldn't move his legs. He felt helpless to do anything. "What sort of...?" He thought of the possibility that this was Druck's doing. If Druck could get into his house, then Druck could find him here. "What sort of trick is this?" he blurted.

The old man's stepped forward. "No trick," he said calmly. "I'm your father."

Aidan finally got the nerve to run. He counted to three in his head, turned as fast as he could, and ran as hard as his legs would take him. When he reached full speed, he turned his head to see if the man was following him, but he was gone. Feeling safe, he slowed down to rest, leaning against a tree to catch his breath.

"You cannot outrun me. Try as you may, I will not leave you."

Aidan stood up and turned around to find the old

man standing behind him. He walked backwards, tripped over a tree root and fell to the ground. "Who are you?" Aidan shouted. He felt like he was losing his mind. "What do you want?"

"I am here to teach you. You have much to learn."

He stood and faced the old man figuring that he'd rather die now than run like a coward anymore. "Show yourself for who you are, Druck!" he demanded.

"I am not Druck. Unfortunately, he serves my brother."

Aidan cocked his head in disbelief. Were it really Druck, he would have most certainly taken credit for this scheme and would have shown himself by now. Suddenly, for whatever reason, a certain peace overcame him. "You said that you were my father."

"Yes. That is because I am."

"But you're a Sarcugian magician."

The old man walked slowly toward Aidan and stopped a few paces from him. "I am the creator."

Aidan took a deep breath. "You're saying that you're God?"

"I am a god. There are several."

"I am only familiar with the one God who controls the universe."

The old man smiled. "Your one true God is but a symbol for all of us."

"Wh...What?"

"Take a walk with me. Like I said, you have much to learn." The old man turned and walked towards the stream. "This is my favorite place to think," he said.

Aidan watched as he walked away. He was too

curious to stay behind, yet he wanted to run. After several seconds, he decided to follow this "god" to find out more. If this was Druck's doing, he'd find out sooner than later.

"I'm so glad you decided to come with me."

"What do I call you?" asked Aidan.

"Oh, I have many names I guess. There is a different name for me in every culture, in every language, and it has changed throughout the ages."

"What is it now?"

"YOU can call me father."

Aidan wanted to grab his robe to spin him around, but he was too afraid. "Why do you keep calling me your son? My father is in the clearing on the other side of the woods."

The old man turned around. "Because I created you from my own body. You are made from me. You are my incarnate flesh."

Aidan felt lightheaded. His heart raced, and he found it difficult to breath. "You mean that you created everyone on earth, and I'm a human, so I'm your child, right?"

"No. Mankind as a whole was created from universal matter. You, my child, were created from MY matter. You are unique. You are me."

He wanted to laugh. This sounded even more preposterous than that story his father told him earlier. "Why in the world would you create me?"

The old man sat down on a stump and extended his hand to Aidan. "Come. Sit, and we shall discuss this. This shall be your first lesson. It is appropriate to begin here."

Aidan reluctantly sat down. This man glowed

like the sun, and when he got close, he could feel the warmth that radiated from his body. For the first time, it felt natural and good to be close to him.

"It all begins with my brother. Many years ago, he became jealous of me. Humanity worshipped me because I gave them magic and healing power. I became the god of all that was good, and he became known as the punisher – the one who brought misfortune. He hated me for that.

"I suppose there was only so much he could take because he tried to defeat me in battle. Once he realized that he could not destroy me, he tried to get the other gods to turn against me, but they would not. His punishment for his effort was exile from our kingdom. In defiance, he made his home here on Earth and has spent all of his energy trying to defeat that which I found to be good.

"He is the source of black magic. He is the source of misery. And his goal is to turn this world into a new kingdom of darkness so that he can fight me once again with his minions by his side."

Aidan turned to the man. He wanted to touch him, but he was still afraid. The story sounded good, but it was too far-fetched for his imagination, and he still wanted to know how he fit into it all. "What about me? Why?"

"A hundred years ago, my brother launched a great war. I did not think he had power over enough humans to see it through. I allowed him complete reign of the Earth to see how loyal and brave my people were. To test them. I gave one man great power. He was unlike any that I had created before, both healer and magician. He was my only defense in case the war went bad. Fortunately, it didn't go bad. My people were victorious on their own. However, I learned a great lesson. Relying upon a human to do my will was wrong. It was too much for him, and he fled here to hide instead of standing against evil."

Aidan opened his eyes wide. "So the legend was true?! He did exist!"

"Yes."

"Does his bloodline continue?"

"No. You nor your friends will find anyone like him."

Aidan's heart sank. He thought about Lord Nilet and Gornia. If there was no hope, then there would most certainly be war, and everyone he knew would be massacred.

"Don't worry. There is hope."

Aidan sat up. "You read my mind?"

"Yes. You will understand everything very soon, I promise."

Aidan felt more comfortable now than he had since he met this man. He wasn't buying the "god" thing, but he thought the man had knowledge that would be useful. Perhaps this was the Healer Magician himself. And maybe this was just a big test.

"But things have changed for the worse ever since. My brother's need to destroy that which I love prompted him to create the most evil, vile creature that has ever set foot on Earth."

"Are you referring to Druck?"

"Yes. He is my brother's flesh."

"I thought he was the son of the last Sarcugian king." Aidan couldn't remember the ruler's name, but he did remember the stories. He'd heard them often over the years.

"My brother seeded the King's wife, and she gave birth to the evil one. Then, he made sure that he taught the boy black magic. He was his son's teacher."

"So how do I fit in?"

The old man stood and faced Aidan. "When I learned of my brother's treachery, I knew that I had to put in place someone who could stop his madness... someone who could defeat Druck. I made the decision that I would take no chances, however, and instead of having a human bare my child, I gave you life from my life. You were born of me."

"What benefit is that? I mean...what's the difference then between me and Druck?" Aidan was patronizing the old man in hopes that he would build a trust so he would finally tell the truth.

"I understand your misgivings, but first, let me answer your question. My brother fathered Druck in earthly fashion. Druck then became a student. He is part god and part man. He can still make mistakes. He can get weak. He can be killed. You are none of that. You do not have to be taught. The power is within you. It always has been. But to keep you safe, I made sure that you would not be aware of any of this until the time was right."

Aidan suddenly felt chilled to the bone. Something the old man said resonated within his consciousness, but he couldn't put his finger on it. He just knew that he needed to hear more. He was still skeptical, but a wave of reality hit home. "How?"

"I placed you in the arms of a trusted servant, and she brought you here as a baby to protect you and to teach you my ways. I didn't count on my brother finding out about you, but he did, and he went after you. We fought again, but I was too weak to defeat him this time."

"Why?"

"Creating you took a lot out of me, and he took advantage of that. I was able to shield you from him, so he didn't find you, and my servant escaped and took you to Gornia to be with a family of my choosing. A family that I knew was pure of heart."

Aidan reflected upon the visions that he had while riding in the desert the day before. The old lady who shielded him underneath the floorboards of that hut, the fire raining down from the sky, the dead bodies…it was all making some sort of sense to him now. That is why he could remember this place.

"Was my father telling the truth when he said I saved that baby a few days ago?"

"I blocked your memory and suppressed your power for as long as I could, but things are bad now, and it was time for you to stand against Druck. Yes, you did that, and you don't remember because I have yet to fully release you. I wanted to personally introduce you to yourself so we could be one."

Aidan ran his fingers through his matted hair. He was numb from confusion and frustration. This had been the worst day of his life, and he wasn't sure if it was getting better or worse. He still didn't know if this was some sort of game initiated by Druck. He wasn't sure of anything.

"Are you ready for your awakening?"

"Are you telling me that I will be able to kill Druck just by snapping my finger?"

The old man shook his head. "I wish it were that

easy. My brother is strong, and he has trained Druck for many years, growing his power far more than I'd like. This is going to be a difficult war, and you will not be able to do it alone. Just as you have my power, Druck has his father's. And you two will lead your people against one another in a great war that will decide the fate of mankind. Were I able, I would fight the fight against my brother for you, but since his exile, I am unable to. This is his only recourse. He cannot fight me in the heavens again, but he can and will fight me here on Earth as he did after you were born. It is now his home, and he wants dominion over all, and I am unwilling to give it to him. To finally defeat him, I must do so through you."

"Can I die then if I am made of you?"

"My brother will not take the risk. He would be bound by the Council and sentenced to an eternity in solitude should he try again. I have seen to that. And not of man's hands, either. But Druck can, and he will try. If that day should come to pass, all things good will be doomed, and Earth will live forever in evil. This is my last stand here on Earth."

Aidan walked a few steps away and pointed in the distance. "And what of my friends and my father? What is to become of them?"

"They have been chosen to help you. Nothing has been by accident."

"How am I supposed to tell them?"

"They will recognize your true self after your awakening. They will believe."

"And Amelia?"

"I know her heart. It will work out well."

"How?!"

"Everything will happen in good time. Now, it is time. Are you ready?"

Aidan closed his eyes tightly. Was he really buying into this? Then he thought about everything that had happened to him today. "I give up...I just give up." He turned and grabbed the old man by the arms. "Let's do it," he said.

A bolt of electricity coursed through his body as he held onto his robe. Images of the heavens opened up before his eyes. Two gods stood side by side and molded a new planet. Primitive humans gathered together and paid homage to their creators. A violent battle between two gods was fought in another world. One god was cast away. Dark clouds swirled over Earth. Evil flourished as black magic grew strong off of the souls of good people. A young baby was born and whisked away by the dark god, trained from an early age to destroy mankind. Another god pulled his heart out and made a baby. He placed it in the arms of an old virgin who cared for him. An earthly battle ensued, fire fell from the sky, and the old lady escaped with the baby. She travelled day and night through exhaustion and starvation to deliver the baby to a man – his father. His mother and father loved him, and they raised him in a loving family. The dark god grew more powerful, and his son grew equally as strong. The son met with an emissary from Gornia and plotted to kill him to provoke the final war. A black fog swirled and everything went black.

Aidan opened his eyes. They were his father's eyes – solid black – the eyes of a god. He looked at his arms and hands, then his legs and the rest of his body. His countenance had changed. He had a soft glow just like his father. He no longer wore the clothes he came in. He was now clothed in the armor of a god, ready for battle. His breastplate and cape were as white as ivory, as were his pants and boots. All things were known to him now. He truly was his father's son.

"You and I are now one once again," his father said. "We will always be together as one in spirit and flesh." He reached up, cupped his son's face with his hand, and smiled. "You will not lose who you were either."

Aidan smiled and closed his eyes. "I know."

His father vanished into thin air.

Chapter 25

Bline and Griswold reached the top of the mountain at dusk after pushing hard through the day to cross the Sarcugian Desert. Griswold didn't understand what all the rush was for, but Bline pushed hard with urgency. He was too afraid to cross the powerful magician again, so he rode in escort blindly following orders. To his great dismay, they spotted Lord Barton's campfire near the stream below the mountain. This wasn't a confrontation he wanted, yet he didn't have a way to get out of it. Gornia's fate, he thought, was partially in his hands.

"We camp here tonight," Bline said as he dismounted his horse.

Griswold looked around. They were surrounded by tall trees and rocks, the only flat land being the path they rode on. "What? Here?"

"Stop your whining, Griswold. We can't risk trying to take them in the dark." He laid a blanket on the ground. "We rise before dawn, and we walk down and surprise them."

"That seems so...mortal," said Griswold. "We should bind them with a spell and then take them."

"You know nothing of what we are dealing with," said Bline. "I'd keep my mouth shut if I were you. Let me do the thinking, you fool."

Griswold had tired of being treated like a peasant. "How do you expect me to understand our mission if you continually keep me in the dark?!"

"Lower your voice, you idiot," said Bline. "It echoes throughout the valley. They do not know we're here, and I would like to keep it that way."

Griswold crouched down. "Tell me the plan, dammit."

Bline rolled onto his side away from him. "You'll know everything you need to know when the time is right. Now go to sleep."

Griswold took a drink from his canteen. What a load of crap, he thought. He unrolled his blanket and laid down on the ground. He could see the glimmer of the campfire below. How Barton could have gotten himself in such a mess, he'd never know.

Dark was approaching fast, and Aidan had yet to return to camp. Geoffrey tried to take his mind off of things by gathering firewood, hoping at any moment that his boy would walk out of the woods. He wanted to go after him. He kept thinking of all the negative things that could have happened. What if he were hurt, or what if he'd been attacked by a wild animal? Was he lost? He certainly didn't expect him to stay in the woods all day, and now that dark has approached, he wished he had gone after him earlier.

Lord Barton and Amelia sat beside the fire and watched the wood burn. It had been a grueling day for Amelia. She fought every last muscle in her body to keep herself from going in after him. She knew that he had some demons to deal with, but not knowing where he was or what his problems were was killing her. She wanted to help him through whatever problems he had, and not being able to be there for him was painful. Waiting for him was more than an exercise in patience, it was torture.

"We should get some sleep, Amelia," said Lord Barton. "Tomorrow will be a busy day."

"You're not thinking of leaving without him," said Amelia. "I mean, what if hasn't returned before then? What are we to do?"

Lord Barton wasn't ready to make a decision. In fact, he didn't want to make it. But what was he supposed to do? This wasn't a camping trip in the wilderness for fun. They had to find this healer magician before Lord Nilet died. He felt that he was already risking Gornia by waiting an extra day, but another day on top of that? Impossible. "What would you have me do?"

"Wait. Wait for him until he comes back. That's what I want you to do." Amelia was getting upset again. She knew that she couldn't leave until Aidan was back.

Lord Barton clinched his fists. "We cannot wait any longer. There are more important things to consider."

Amelia stood up. "Like what? Your pride? Your stubbornness? Your resolve to get your mission accomplished?"

"That's not fair!" he shouted. "Have you forgotten the thousands of people who will die if we do not succeed?! They're not numbers! Our people will be mowed down! Fathers, mothers, children...all dead! And for what? One person who walks out on his friends because he has a problem that he needs to deal with?! Think about what you're saying!"

He stood and walked into the shadows. He was tired of dealing with Aidan and wished he'd never brought him along. "Useless," he muttered. "What a useless piece of garbage."

Amelia cried. She would fight her brother with everything she had to stay, but deep down, she knew he was right. She was being selfish, and she knew it. She loved Aidan so much and didn't want to lose him, especially this way. But there was more at stake than just one person, and she couldn't live knowing that she caused Gornia to fall all because she loved one man.

Sunrise came earlier than anyone wanted. The air was cooler than it had been the previous two days since they'd arrived, and it looked like a storm front was moving in around the peaks of the mountains.

Lord Barton went to the stream to splash his face. When he got to the water, he looked around at the forest on the other side of the river. Then he turned, and looked in the direction where Aidan had left the morning before.

"Is there something wrong?" asked Geoffrey. He bent down to fill his canteen.

Lord Barton cupped the cold water and splashed it against his face, rubbing his eyes vigorously to get the sleep out. "Listen," he said.

Geoffrey stood. It was silent. The birds weren't chirping, deer weren't prancing through the woods, and even the stream didn't sound as bubbly as it had before. "That's odd," said Geoffrey. He walked up the stream bank and slowly turned around. "It's too quiet."

"Yes it is." Lord Barton ran towards the camp to

wake Amelia. "Get up," he yelled.

"What?" She slowly sat up and rubbed her eyes. "What's the hurry?"

"Someone's out there," he said. He slowly scanned the horizon. They were caught between two mountains, and it was impossible to see who was watching them from this point of view. There were just too many trees and rocks.

Geoffrey ran up. "What do you think is going on?"

Amelia got up and put on her boots. Her heart raced. "Who is it?"

Lord Barton scanned the horizon. "It's not good," he said. He looked up. Dark clouds swirled overhead and grew more intense than ever. "Druck."

Amelia gasped. "Druck? How does he know we're here?"

"He's probably looking for the same person we are," said Geoffrey.

A cold gust of wind blew through the valley, bending the tree tops like tiny saplings.

"What do we do?" Amelia shouted.

"I don't know," said Lord Barton. He wanted to mount up and ride off, but he knew that Druck would catch them sooner than later, and the footing wouldn't be good on those old mountain roads. They'd have no chance to defend themselves if they got attacked up there. But if they stayed, they'd have to face him here and now, and he wasn't sure that he was prepared to do that either.

Geoffrey pointed to a large boulder on the other side of the village. "Let's move behind that rock for cover," he yelled. "We can hide there until we figure out what's going on!"

A bolt of lightning flashed from the dark cloud overhead striking a tree on the other side of the stream. The wind picked up and blew hard enough to snap the top off another tree just a few paces from their camp.

Amelia ran for the horses. "Leave them!" shouted Geoffrey. "They're just as safe where they are than with us!"

"Let me at least untie them!"

Lord Barton grabbed her arm. "Don't! We'll need them when this is done!"

Amelia reluctantly followed the two men to the other side of the old village. The boulder was large enough for them to hide behind, but it made it impossible to see if anyone was coming towards them from the mountain.

Bline and Griswold stood in the tree line at the edge of the village no more than two hundred paces from the boulder. Bline pointed a finger towards the clouds and then drew it down like a sword towards a tree near the boulder. A bolt of lightning streaked out of the cloud and struck the tree midway down the trunk causing it to break in half and fall. A small branch struck Lord Griswold's back but didn't hurt him.

"Look at those cowards," chuckled Bline. "They think that rock can save them."

"I thought there were four," said Griswold. "I only see three."

Bline took a deep breath. "The other is in the woods. I will take care of him myself. These three are yours."

Griswold shook his head. "How am I supposed to take care of them? I don't know how to use my power."

Bline turned to Griswold and grabbed the amulet and pushed it into his face. "Look into the stone!"

Griswold pushed back, but Bline had him pinned against a tree and pushed harder. The amulet was crushing the young magician's face. Bline pulled in close. "Look into the damn stone. You've always wanted power, wealth, and prestige, well I'm about to give it to you."

Griswold looked away, but Bline grabbed his head and pulled it forward. "Don't tell me you don't want it now. This is your father's wish, and it's mine too. Take it! Enjoy your new life and savor the fact that you'll be doing Gornia a huge favor!"

Griswold glanced into the emerald. The flashes of lightning coursed through the stone faster and faster until two bolts shot into his eyes. Griswold gasped for air as the stone took control of him. His legs were the first to shake, and then his arms. A few seconds later, his entire body went into convulsions and he fell to the ground. After a minute, he stopped shaking, and his body went limp.

Bline reached down and felt his neck. "Good boy," he said. "I knew you had what it takes. He picked the magician up and leaned him against the tree. Griswold wiped his mouth and opened his eyes slowly. They burned like fire. Black magic had filled his soul. He was now one of them.

Griswold smiled. The power that flowed through his body felt good. He was energized and ready to stop anyone who stood in his way. "I know what to do," he told Bline calmly. "I'll take care of these three. You can have the other one."

Bline smiled. Now he didn't have to put up with Griswold, the lame fool, anymore. He reached his arms towards the clouds, closed his eyes, and vanished. Griswold turned and saw that he had left. "Time to hunt the prey," he said, and he walked out of the tree line into open view.

"Sulfur," said Lord Barton. He turned to Amelia. "Do you smell that?"

She took several deep breaths through her nose. The familiar odor got her attention. "Yea." She sounded concerned.

Geoffrey smelled the air too. He recognized the smell but didn't understand what it meant. "What's the matter?" he asked.

"Magician's can transport themselves upon occasion," he said.

Amelia turned to Geoffrey. "It takes a lot of energy and concentration, but it can be done."

"Only powerful magicians can do it without consequence," added Lord Barton.

Geoffrey looked at the ground and thought. "So we must be dealing with someone pretty powerful then. I mean, if he's transporting to fight us, right?"

"That's what we're afraid of," said Amelia.

"Lord Barton?" asked Geoffrey.

"Yes."

"Without being disrespectful…" he paused.

"Go ahead, Geoffrey," said Lord Barton. He pointed towards the sky. "Now's not the time for me to take offense."

"How confident are you that you can hold your

ground?"

Lord Barton took a deep breath. "I'll do my best." He looked at Amelia and put his hand on her arm. "We can do this."

Amelia shook her head. "I can't do anything, and you know it."

"You have to help me. We might have to combine our powers."

"Powers? I'm still an apprentice. I don't have any power."

He tapped the side of her head. "It's all in there. You just have to use it."

"I don't know how to use it," she said. "I've been a failure as a magician. You know that." She turned back to look at the woods where Aidan left. For the first time, she was glad he wasn't here.

"Look up!" cried Lord Barton.

Geoffrey and Amelia looked towards the sky. The dark clouds were breaking apart, and the sun started to shine again. The wind gradually faded into a gentle breeze.

"Maybe he left," said Geoffrey.

Amelia grabbed her brother's arm. "That smell... perhaps he did leave. That makes perfect sense."

"Barton!"

Lord Barton turned to Geoffrey and Amelia. "Did you hear that?"

"I heard something, but I couldn't make it out," said Geoffrey.

"Barton!" The voice grew louder.

Lord Barton let out a deep breath of air. "That sounds like Griswold. It can't be!" He got to his feet and squatted behind the rock.

Amelia grabbed his thigh. "Don't! It could be a trick!" Her heart was pounding. Someone stayed, and she didn't have a good feeling about it.

"Barton! Are you there?!"

"By God, it is Griswold!" said Lord Barton. He stood and exposed his position to his friend. He could see him walking down the road at the other end of the village street. "What in God's name are you doing here, you old crow?!" He had never been happier to see a familiar face.

Amelia and Geoffrey weren't so sure about this, so they stayed behind the rock, cautiously watching Lord Barton as he stepped out into the opening.

"I met with the Emperor," Griswold said. "And he sent me to come for you!"

Lord Barton came within thirty paces of his friend when he noticed something wrong. His eyes were red. He stopped in his tracks and froze. "Black magic," he mumbled. "What in the world?" He turned around and motioned for Geoffrey and Amelia to stay right where they were.

"What's the matter, old friend?" asked Griswold. "I've come all this way to help you, and you don't greet me as a friend?" He stopped about ten paces in front of Lord Barton and stared.

Lord Barton was pale, and a cold sweat rolled off his forehead.

Griswold laughed. "Oh…it must be the eyes," he said. "The women love them! What's say I ask your lovely sister?"

Lord Barton raised a hand to tell him no, but it was too late. Griswold raised his finger in the air.

"What's happening?!" screamed Amelia.

Lord Barton turned around to see his sister lifting off the ground and starting to levitate towards them. Geoffrey grabbed her ankles to try to pull her back to the rock, but Griswold swatted him back, throwing him to the ground several paces from the stone.

"Griswold! Have you gone mad?" screamed Lord Barton.

"Not at all," chuckled Griswold. "I just thought I'd find out if she liked my new look. After all, she will have to like it because I am going to make her mine!"

He brought her to the ground several inches in front of him. He stroked her red hair and sighed. "You are just as beautiful as I remember."

"Let me go you pig!" she screamed. She pulled back, but the more she pulled, the closer he brought her in. "You stink of black magic," she said, and then she spit into his face.

Griswold wiped his mouth and sneered. "You bitch!" he screamed. He struck her in the head with the back of his hand. "How dare you! You will learn to respect me!"

Lord Barton ran to his sister. But, before he could get within five paces, Griswold picked him up and threw him violently to the ground. He slowly crawled to his knees as blood streaked down his face from and dripped to the ground. "Explain yourself, you Bastard!" he yelled.

Griswold stared down his old friend. "Piss off, you ass. As if you ever gave a damn about me!"

Geoffrey stood near the rock and looked at Lord Barton. He didn't know what to do. He wanted to help, but he knew that he would be killed the minute he dared confront the madman.

Amelia couldn't move under Griswold's power but she could speak. "You're nothing but a coward. You could never have been a good magician, so what do you do? You turn to black magic. What good are you?" She hoped she'd make him angry enough to turn his attention back on her so her brother would have a chance to do something.

"You are a dirty little girl, aren't you?" He pointed at her blouse and raked his finger through the air, tearing the garment from her body and exposing her breast. He licked his lips.

"Don't you dare touch me, you animal," she hissed. She prayed that she could break his hold on her, but everything she tried failed.

Lord Barton reached forward with both arms and yanked back quickly. Griswold was thrown hard to the ground on his back and was pulled towards Lord Barton in a cloud of dust. Amelia fell to the ground immediately after being released from his spell. She put her shirt on and ran to Geoffrey as quickly as she could.

Griswold slid to Lord Barton's feet, laughing hard when he came to a stop. "Good one!" he shouted.

"Not as good as this." Lord Barton raised Griswold from the ground and threw him into a tree, bending his body around the trunk like a piece of paper. "Leave my sister alone!" he shouted. He turned to Amelia. "Are you alright?" But the look in her eyes gave it away. He turned around and barely had a second to deflect a ball of fire harmlessly into the stream. His protective shield glistened in the sunlight as he held it for a few seconds to make sure another wasn't heading his way.

Griswold stood at the base of the tree enjoying the game that he played with the two weak magicians. "Should I just put you out of your misery now, or would it be better if I kept you around a little while longer for fun?" he pondered aloud. "Well, I must say that I'm enjoying this little rendezvous. I don't think I'm ready to go home yet, so let's play!"

Amelia closed her eyes and pointed her hand towards Griswold. A stream of fire poured from her palm and engulfed him in flames. When she looked up, Griswold simply smiled at her. There were no singes on his body whatsoever.

"Is that the best you can do?" he mocked. "Come on! I could do better than that when I was a child!" He looked at Lord Barton. "Your turn," he said. "Go ahead. I won't stop you. But make sure it's good."

Lord Barton stomped his foot on the ground. It shook violently and a large crack zigzagged towards Griswold. The earth opened up and swallowed him whole before closing back up. "I bet you weren't counting on that!" said Lord Barton.

Amelia and Geoffrey ran to him. "Great job!" cried Amelia as she embraced him. "I never heard about that one!"

"Father taught it to me before he died."

Geoffrey patted him on the back. "I had faith in…" He stopped before he could finish. "Did you feel that?"

The ground started to tremble. It shook so hard that he lost his balance and fell. "What's going on?!" he cried.

"It must be Griswold!" shouted Lord Barton. "I thought that would have finished him off!"

The ground exploded. Dirt and stone struck the three as they shielded their faces from the debris. As the dust settled, they could see a bloodied Griswold hovering over the cavern below.

"Good job Barton," said Griswold. "I wasn't expecting that at all!" He set himself down at the edge of the hole. "Now, it's my turn!"

Chapter 26

Aidan sat on the stone that marked the spot where the Earth was created. He spent the time alone to meditate upon his new life as the God of Magic and Healing. Born a god, raised as a human, he carried the best of both in him. And in this role, he would serve mankind well by ridding the world of all that was destructive. Good could only be served once evil had been stamped out, and as his father told him, that was his role to fulfill.

"I have been expecting you," Aidan said without turning around. He knew who was there. He could feel his presence from legions away.

"Your friends are battling for their lives right now," said Baul, his voice filled with the screams of lost souls. "Why haven't you come to their assistance?"

"I know their plight," Aidan said. "I see them now."

"And you don't fear for their lives?"

Aidan stood and faced the dark god. "Exile hasn't gone well for you, I see," he said. "You are so ugly now."

Baul laughed. "You speak like my brother. Has he fooled you into believing he made you from his own body? I hope not because I would hate to see the look in your eyes when I kill you."

"You cannot kill me," Aidan said. "You want to, but you know that you cannot."

Baul walked towards him confidently. "Oh, but I can. You're nothing more than a little orphan boy in a white suit. I can kill you, and I will."

Aidan held his hand up, stopping Baul from getting any closer to him. "You've spent too much time pretending to be Bline," he said. "You're starting to believe your own lies."

Baul pushed against Aidan's power but could not move closer. He shook his head and chuckled. "You are my brother's son, aren't you? I should have killed you when you were a baby."

"Oh, you tried. I remember it well. I can still smell your stench. I thought it was the burning flesh of those innocents you slaughtered, but it was always you that I smelled, wasn't it?"

"The Council may prevent me from killing you, but they cannot stop my son."

"That must hurt."

Baul laughed. "What must hurt?"

"Knowing that your son will die at my hand one day."

Baul lurched forward but pulled back before going too far. "You insolent fool! It will be you who dies at his hand!"

Aidan turned and sat on the stone with his back facing Baul. "Why is it that you came to me rather than your son?"

"I came to make you an offer," he said. "I will give you equal dominion over all of this land if you join me."

"And serve beside Druck?"

"Yes."

Aidan laughed. "You wasted your time then."

"Then you leave me no choice. I will tell Druck that you exist, and he will hunt you down until you are dead."

"Is that so? I welcome him here right now. We can end this without any more bloodshed."

Baul's eyes turned as red as the burning sun. "You will regret this decision. I promise you."

Aidan turned and stared at Baul. "Your days are numbered, Baul. Enjoy them while you can."

Baul screamed in anger, and then he vanished.

Amelia and Geoffrey watched in horror as Griswold held Lord Barton high in the air while choking him. Her brother frantically reached for his throat trying to counter whatever magic that was restricting his breath.

"Suffocation is an agonizing death from what I hear," mocked Griswold. He turned to Amelia. "Come to me and I will release him from my grip."

Amelia didn't know what to do. She knew that her brother would be dead no matter what she did, but she also knew that Griswold could force her to come if she didn't want to. She had no choice, so she started walking towards him. "I'm coming," she said. "Let him go."

Griswold closed his hand tighter causing Lord Barton to wheeze more.

"I said I am coming!" she yelled. "Please release him."

As soon as she stood beside him, he turned to her. "Do you want me to give him a slow death, or should I just break his neck right now?"

Amelia fell to her knees. "Please don't hurt him. Please."

"What the…" Griswold looked at Amelia. "What are you doing?"

She looked and saw that he was putting her brother on the ground.

"Are you mocking me?!" shouted Griswold. "How did you release your brother?!" He backhanded her on the side of the face and knocked her to the ground."

Lord Barton laid on the ground and tried to catch his breath. Geoffrey ran to his side and held him up.

"You're finished Griswold!" said Aidan.

Griswold swung around. He found him standing on the boulder that the three had hidden behind earlier. "What is this? Some kind of trick?" laughed Griswold. "You're nothing but a boy!"

Amelia pushed herself off the ground. Griswold had hit her so hard that she could not see clearly. She looked towards the stone but couldn't make out who was there. The voice sounded so familiar, but it was different. It sounded like the ocean. She tried to stand, but she fell back to the ground dizzy.

Geoffrey and Lord Barton froze. It looked like Aidan, but he was different.

"You will die," said Aidan. "Shall I snap your neck now or should I make you suffer? The choice is yours."

Griswold reached back and threw a massive fireball at Aidan. "It crashed hard into the boulder and exploded into thousands of embers. "That should take care of you!"

"Is that all you've got?"

Griswold turned around. Aidan was now standing behind him. "How did you do that?!" cried Griswold.

He reached up and turned his hand in the air. A large bolt of lightning struck from the sky and hit Aidan on top of the head. He didn't flinch as the electricity passed through him.

Amelia pulled herself to Aidan's feet. He picked her up and held her in his arms. She was still stunned from Griswold's blow. "Aidan, is that you?" she said. A trickle of blood rolled down her neck from a gash in her head. Aidan touched the wound, and healed it. "Yes, it's me," he said softly. "I'm here."

She smiled. "I'm so glad..." She passed out before she could finish.

Aidan laid her gently on the ground and turned his attention to Griswold. "What else have you got for me?"

Griswold's eyes burned with rage. "How dare you toy with me!"

"As you toyed with them?"

Griswold leaned back and threw his arms behind him. He summoned his powers from the deepest corners of his soul. The wind started to blow hard, a dark cloud appeared overhead, and a tornado dropped over Aidan and returned to the cloud in a flash. When he looked, Aidan was gone. He started laughing. "And you thought I was weak!"

"You are."

Griswold spun around once more to find Aidan staring at him. He stumbled back. "Your eyes..." he said. "They're the eyes of a god." He fell backwards and tried to shuffle away from Aidan as quickly as he could.

Geoffrey squinted his eyes to see what Griswold was seeing. Aidan's eyes were like coal, just like the day he saw him deliver that baby. He knew there was something to it.

"I am a god. I am the god who will execute you."

Griswold threw his hands over his face. "No! No!" His skin started to melt off his body. In a matter of seconds, his skeleton was all that remained, and even it crumbled to dust.

Aidan picked the amulet off the ground and crushed it in his hand, shattering it into hundreds of pieces. "Pity that the poor soul was tricked so easily."

Geoffrey and Lord Barton staggered towards Aidan and knelt at his feet. "Thank you, my Lord," said Lord Barton. He still didn't know what to make of all this, but he knew that Aidan was more than he would ever be.

"Stand," said Aidan. He held out his arms and hugged them both. "I am sorry you had to endure him for so long."

Geoffrey broke down in tears. "I thought I had lost you forever."

Aidan pulled him tightly to his side. He then looked down at Amelia. "We have a lot to talk about," he said.

Chapter 27

Amelia woke with the sensation of a thousand butterflies fluttering over her body. She looked up and saw Aidan. As soon as she got a good look at him, she pushed back as hard as she could to get away. His eyes scared her the most. She'd never seen anything so black before in her life. And his skin glowed softly, lighting the shade of the tree he placed her under. After all she had been through today, she was sure that he had been infected with black magic just like Griswold.

"Don't be afraid," said Lord Barton. He leaned behind her and helped her get off the ground. "Aidan saved us."

As she stood, she stared at the man she used to love. "I...I don't understand," she said. "What happened to you?"

Aidan stepped towards her with open arms, but she pulled back and huddled in her brother's arms. "It is still me," said Aidan.

"But...your eyes," she paused as she gathered her thoughts. "Your voice...what's happened to you?"

"I know it's a lot to take in, Amelia. I, above all, understand your fears...your concerns." He turned to Geoffrey to welcome him into the group with an open arm. "I have a lot to explain." He nodded his head and smiled. "And when I have finished, it will all make sense."

Geoffrey stepped towards Lord Barton and Amelia so he could face Aidan. He shook his head. "I knew something special was at work in you since you delivered Tessera's child, but I had no idea that you would become..." He didn't know how to finish his sentence.

"A god," Aidan injected.

"A god?" Lord Barton asked. His mouth gaped open as he pondered what Aidan said.

Aidan motioned to the ground. "Please sit, and I will explain."

When they turned around to find a spot on the ground to sit, they noticed three flat stones behind them. "How did he do that?" Amelia asked her brother. He shook his head in disbelief and helped her to a stone.

"I hope you are now comfortable," said Aidan.

Amelia looked closely at Aidan's clothes and armor. They were as white as fresh snow with the exception of the gold trim around his cape.

"My earthly mother and father raised me well in love and happiness. I wanted for nothing, and I was treated as their own. But they knew I was not of their flesh.

"My real father is Ursus, and he created me from his own heart and placed me here on Earth to destroy the growing evil we are facing today."

Lord Barton recognized the name Ursus, but he couldn't remember how he knew it. He thought hard until he remembered. "I know of Ursus," he said. "Our ancestors used to worship him. He was the God of..." He stopped because he couldn't remember which god he was.

"He and his brother Baul created our world. Many years ago, they fought over control of Earth. Baul was exiled to spend eternity on Earth. He vowed then to destroy all that my father loved about humanity.

"He had a son that we know as Druck, and his plan is to use Druck to bring Earth and all humans under his control. That is why my father created me. It is my responsibility to defeat Druck and Baul, so this world can have peace forever."

Amelia couldn't believe what she was hearing. Three days ago, the man standing in front of her was an apprentice healer who she grew up with and loved. Now he was telling her that he was a god? She closed her eyes and shook her head. She just knew that he had gone insane.

Aidan looked at her. "I could not tell you any of this because I did not know myself. My father closed my mind and body to my true self until we met here. Druck's power grows by the day, and it was time to let me loose."

"Why here?" asked Amelia. "Why not in Heshire while Druck prepared his plans?"

"My father led us here so he could reveal my identity to me where it all began. This place is where Earth was created. As well, he needed to protect me from Baul. Had Baul known who I was, he would have killed me, and I was not prepared to face him until now."

"So there is no healer magician?" asked Lord Barton.

"There was. It was my father's first attempt to bring peace. But he was too human to do what was needed, and he fled here many years ago, dying in seclusion. To defeat Druck and Baul, a god is required to do the work. It cannot be left to human hands alone. We cannot expect a human to do a god's work."

"And what are we to do?" asked Geoffrey. He was

not nearly as dumbfounded as Lord Barton and Amelia. He always had a feeling that Aidan was special, and during the past week, he saw that he was more than just a mere mortal. A god? He didn't think that would be the outcome, but he knew Aidan was more than a healer.

"Nothing has happened by chance. Your lives have been planned accordingly. Do not underestimate the job at hand. It will be a difficult and trying war, and I will need you to stand with me."

Amelia got up and ran towards the woods as hard as she could. She didn't want them to see her cry. She didn't need compassion right now. She needed to be alone. She no longer thought Aidan was mad, and she didn't believe this was the product of black magic. But gods and wars? It was too much for her to process. All she wanted was for her old Aidan to grow old together. She wanted things to be the same as they were. She wanted to look into his human eyes, hear his human voice, and caress his human skin. All of that had been taken away from her, and she hated this Ursus for allowing her to fall in love with his son. She ran deep into the woods until she could run no more, and she fell to her face and sobbed.

"There is no need to cry," said Aidan.

She looked up and wiped her face with her arm. Aidan was standing over her. "How did you…?"

"I still love you as I did. Nothing has changed."

She pushed to her knees and threw a handful of rotting leaves at him. "How?!" she screamed. "If you are a god, how can we love one another?!"

"I am flesh as I am spirit," he replied. "I am as I always was."

"You're different!" she exclaimed. "I hardly recognize you!"

"I am fully born now," he said, "but I am the same as you knew." He reached out with his hand and helped her to her feet. "I need you by my side now as much as I ever did."

She looked at him through tear-swollen eyes. "I love you so much," she said.

"I love you too. I always will."

Geoffrey and Lord Barton saddled their horses in preparation for their journey back to Heshire. There was much work to be done to prepare for a war with Druck. Lord Barton needed to get to Tarsus with Lord Nilet before the next moon to inform him of Druck's intentions.

"So Lord Nilet is recovering?" asked Lord Barton. He'd asked Aidan this question three times throughout the morning to make sure he heard right.

"Yes. I have made sure of that. He's getting his strength back as we speak with help from Annabel's cooking."

Geoffrey tied his blanket to the back of his saddle. "Are you sure you can't return with us? He wanted Aidan to come back with him. He didn't care if he wasn't his real son. He was still his boy, and no one could take that away from him.

"I will be there often. Don't worry about that. You will tire of me before it is over."

Geoffrey grinned.

Aidan reached over and embraced him. "You will

be rewarded for your love. Mother already has been. Don't you worry."

He smiled as he thought about his wife. "I will see her again someday," he said.

"She will be there with open arms when you make that last journey."

Geoffrey patted him on the arm. "I still expect you to help me with difficult patients!"

"All you have to do is ask."

Lord Barton hugged Amelia. "Are you sure you want to stay?"

She kissed his cheek. "Yes. This is where I belong."

"Our uncle will be distraught that you won't finish your apprenticeship with him," chuckled Lord Barton. "But who better to learn from than the source of all magic?"

She smiled. "We will have a beautiful life together. He is going to create an oasis for us to live in. It's going to be beautiful," she said.

"Why can't you return with us and live in Heshire?" Lord Barton asked Aidan.

"People will gather, and they will worship me. It will take their focus off of the war. I cannot let that happen. When we visit, we will visit as one of their own. Remember to keep our truth hidden until it is time."

"We will," said Lord Barton.

"And when I am needed, I will be there. Anytime, anywhere."

They climbed into their saddles and rode towards the mountain road. Geoffrey looked back one last time and waved goodbye. "You are a healer after all," he said. "You'll heal the world."

Baul appeared in Druck's private chamber as Druck bathed. Four naked women massaged his body with oil as he laid in the small pool.

"You pamper yourself too much," said Baul.

Druck turned and looked behind him. He pushed the women off of him and stood naked in front of his father. "Get out!" he shouted to the women as he waved his hand towards the door.

The women scampered out of the pool and ran for the door, closing it as they left.

"I wish you would knock before you entered," he told his father.

Baul stood and walked towards his naked son. His sooty skin staining the towel he handed him. "I wish you would take this more seriously."

Druck laughed. "Why be so serious when I can run them through without raising a finger?"

Baul grabbed Druck by the throat and squeezed. Druck's skin burned from his father's touch. Baul took a breath and released his grip. "Sometimes you frustrate me, son," he said.

Druck rubbed his throat. "What seems to be the problem, father?"

"That waste of life failed to kill the three from Heshire, and Ursus' son has been awakened."

"You know this for sure?" Druck walked to a table by the pool and drank wine from his goblet.

"Of course I know this for sure!" shouted Baul. "I spoke to him myself!"

Druck wiped his face with his towel. "Then I shall just have to kill him." He held the goblet to his mouth and swallowed the last of the wine in one gulp.

"I have only come to warn you," said Baul. "He is very powerful."

Druck turned around. "And so am I! You have made that very clear to me over the years." He reached his arms towards the ceiling. "And I've never felt stronger!"

"Just don't take him lightly," said Baul, and he vanished into the shadows.

Druck grabbed his goblet and threw it into the wall. "We'll see who's victorious!" he shouted. "We'll see!"

www.ingramcontent.com/pod-product-compliance
Lightning Source LLC
Chambersburg PA
CBHW071141170626
46809CB00002B/711